BACK TO YOU

BELLA FONTAINE
KHARDINE GRAY

BACK TO YOU

USA Today Bestselling Author

Khardine Gray

Writing
as

Bella Fontaine

CHAPTER 1

LANA

"Head up. I want the camera to catch your cheek-bones," I instructed Ichika.

She straightened up, trying to achieve the pose I wanted but it wasn't quite right.

She was beautiful and modelled my clothes well. There was just something missing from what I'd wanted her to do.

I rose from my chair and walked onto the set where I had her standing in the center of a rose garden.

Amongst the beautiful arrangement of royal blue long stemmed roses I'd had dyed and made for this shoot, she looked stunning wearing the evening gown I designed as part of my Kiss of Mortality collection.

"Here, focus on this," I suggested, pointing to the blue macaw on the mural to the left of us.

It was one of my favorite things to look at in this studio, simply for the fact that it was beautiful and evoked the senses. Anyone looking at it, no matter how many times you saw it would always get that look of awe and wonder.

I'd had it placed there because it brought a taste of the tropics to *D'Angelo,* my fashion house that was smack in between Santa Monica and en-route to Hollywood. Life around us couldn't be any busier than it was.

Ichika did as I said and a twinkle sparked in her almond shaped eyes when she saw me smile.

The simple switch in focus to the mural had achieved the look I'd wanted. Now, her head was lifted at the perfect angle and her long, slick, black hair hung perfectly over her shoulder blades.

Perfect.

Yes, now she was perfect.

"I like that," Carl nodded with a wide grin of admiration for my instructions. He

was my creative director and right hand man. He knew how I wanted my designs to be portrayed.

"Great, keep it going guys, try and wrap this up in an hour." I signaled Pierre, my photographer, to carry on shooting and I returned to my chair.

We'd all been hard at work since four a.m. On a roll with amazing results.

I'd accepted long ago that I'd fully immersed the fast paced Lifestyle L.A. had to offer. As like you were expected to follow the norm when in Rome, I'd done the same with L.A.

It was so different to Wilmington, the city where I grew up in North Carolina.

I gave Carl my thumbs up when he looked over to me. Ichika definitely rocked the dress and the look I was going for. Carl knew that too. The man knew his stuff and was a perfect addition to my team who'd not only help launch my clothing line but also open the fashion house.

I had a great team and it helped that we shared the zeal for perfection.

Sometimes though, like today, the zeal for perfection took up a little more time

than I liked. It didn't go hand in hand with a busy schedule.

I rested against the leather back of the chair continuing to watch. I'd be the last to admit when I was tired. It seemed however that I wouldn't need to admit anything today because exhaustion had come for me.

Sometimes I couldn't believe how busy I was.

I lived and predominantly worked in L.A but it wasn't uncommon for me to be in New York one day and spend the next day in London or Japan, or God even Bora Bora. I couldn't keep up with myself.

I'd just gotten back from a month long trip to Brazil yesterday morning and it was straight to work to prep for the fashion show I was hosting here at the end of the month. This photoshoot was part of the advertising campaign.

Currently the guest list was a hundred people, and all those people were the cream of the crop in the fashion world. The plan was a series of shows in the buildup to Fashion Week.

I guess it came all part and parcel of my dreams of being a fashion designer. Couldn't have everything smooth sailing. I had to take the good parts with the bad too. It was a good thing the good parts mostly outweighed the bad.

I should have felt happier, and definitely give myself more credit since I'd exceeded the vision of what I'd wanted for myself. In my dreams growing up I'd wanted to work for big designers like Dior, Chanel, Versace and Galliano. I'd done all of that and lived the dream. Never factored in, however, that I could aim higher and be on par with my own brand.

Lana D'Angelo.

That was me. The name I gave myself and my brand.

I'd launched last year when I left Dior and took off like a rocket with my designs and recognition. Then there was the travelling. I liked getting involved with every aspect, so I was always at the photoshoots, always in meetings with fashion magazines and the buyers who took care of my clothing in all the stores and boutiques. Always doing everything.

Mama would have been so proud of me. So proud.

I hoped that she was smiling down on me from heaven, seeing that I'd made it through the vicious storms life had tossed me. For a long time I knew there was no way she could rest in peace.

My life suggested I was okay now. More than okay with my multimillion dollar brand. At thirty-five years old, I was a wealthy, extremely successful, award winning fashion designer.

I'd made it to the dream. I'd never guessed that could happen to a girl like me who came from nowhere and had to build from the ground up.

Maybe I was thinking in *maybes* because every time I thought of my success I imagined life to be different and Mama right next to me. I was still so lost without her.

Lost, and honestly what I'd classed as keeping my head above water.

I was at the pinnacle of my career, and always imagined having her share it with me. That part of me never healed when death took her away. The way it did too was something that would always leave a hole in my soul. The kind of hole and void that nothing could fill.

Movement on the balcony caught my attention and pulled me from my thoughts.

Georgie. Oh goodness, she was waiting for me.

Waiting patiently. I'd rescheduled lunch three times already today. A quick glance at my watch showed she would have been waiting at least fifteen minutes. I'd completely lost track of the time.

Thank God she was used to me. My best friend also happened to have the patience of a saint. I motioned to her and mouthed 'sorry'. She gave me a salute back in her usual good-natured way and I chuckled.

Looking back to the guys on set, I gave a quick scan of what they were doing. They were more than good to continue without me. Everything was as it should be and Carl was rocking this shoot like nobody's business. There was no need to encourage my addiction to perfection by hanging around any longer and not taking a break.

Lunch was calling me along with some much needed girl time with Georgie.

I made my way up to her on the balcony, planning for a fattening lunch first to make up for the dinner and breakfast I'd missed. When I got back I planned to immerse myself into the glorious world of admin for the rest of the day. I had a ton of contracts to sign off.

Georgie smiled at me first then made a show of placing her hands on her hips, pretending to be annoyed.

I laughed at her.

I hadn't seen her in a month and I was eager to catch up properly.

"I'm so sorry, Georgie. God. Time got away from me." I giggled.

"Yes, like always." She shook her head at me and the ends of her salon-perfect hair bounced with life.

"No, no, not like always. Just today and recently. The months before weren't so bad."

Georgie laughed. "Come here, give me some sugar. I missed your late ass." She stretched her arms out and I fell into her embrace.

"I missed you too," I bubbled, hugging her hard. She was like family to me. Just like family. Like a sister. She'd been a great friend. The kind you know you'll always have.

We pulled apart and I looked her over, smiling and loving the fact that my friend looked so good. The newly married Georgina Flynn looked like a million dollars.

This was what six months of marriage did to her. It made her look more fabulous than she already was. I could definitely see that her husband, Pat, was treating her right. As expected. That man spoiled her rotten and I loved that she'd found a guy who deserved her. Granted it took him awhile to notice that she could be more than just his trusty P.A, slash best friend.

It was beyond me how they didn't realize they were in love with each other the whole time she'd worked for him. But such was life.

Now look at her. Georgie could have easily passed for Naomi Campbell on the runway, with her rich dark skin, sass and sexiness.

I was proud that most people mistook us for sisters sometimes, because we looked similar with our style and features. Today though, I was sure people wouldn't make that mistake because I looked so rough.

"Please tell me you intend to take the full hour, Miss Lady," she intoned.

"Absolutely." I gave her my trademark one shoulder sassy shrug. "And I'm in the mood for a double cheese burger and a triple chocolate milkshake, so we might need to head to Bob's Diner."

"Yay, come on, let's go."

I knew that would make her happy. Just the mention of that place and Georgie would forgive me for anything. She skipped closer to me and linked her arm with mine. We then proceeded out to the corridor.

"So how is Pat treating you?" I gave her a curious

grin. It used to be that I was the one with the guy gossip. Since she got together with Pat, nothing I did came close to gossip worthy. I was more interested in hearing about her.

"The man is insufferable, Lana. Now he's talking about kids." She widened her eyes at me.

I gasped. "Georgina Flynn that better not be your way of subtly trying to tell me you're pregnant."

She gave me a bashful smile. The same kind she used to give me back in college.

She did marketing and had the charismatic presence to go with it, but really she was shy as anything.

"No, but I think this is the start of us trying." She chuckled.

"Trying for a baby," I bubbled bringing my hands together with excitement. "Look at you. I'm so proud. That's exciting news." It was and I was genuinely happy for her.

"I think so. Thank you Lana."

She'd gotten married. I had my career. It was supposed to be a win-win situation. People often asked me if I ever had plans to settle down and the short answer would always be yes. The long answer was one I would never attempt to give.

People assumed that my free spirited dating was down to being busy and they were right to a great extent.

But… that was because they didn't know me.

If I had someone who loved me as much as Pat loved Georgie, he would be my number one. I'd just accepted that what she had was rare and not everyone could have it.

The heart was complicated. It hung on to things it shouldn't sometimes. If it had something good once, it was hard to replace it. Especially when you had to give it up.

That was my theory. That was how I assessed myself. How I coped and what I told myself to make the past okay.

I was happy with my work and that was enough. It had to be.

Georgie started talking about her garden as we verged toward the top floor.

Just before we turned to get into the elevator, Winter called me.

She rushed up to us carrying a large folder under her arm and an annoyed look spread over her face.

"Lana, I'm sorry, I know your busy," she said in a rush.

"Just going to lunch," I told her so she wouldn't feel like she'd disturbed me.

She was always apologizing for doing so, which bordered on every time she either saw or spoke to me because I was always busy.

Winter blew out a ragged breath. "Can it wait? There is a really rude man in your office. I was going to call security or even the police with the way he was going on, but I didn't want to cause any drama."

Hearing that someone had been so rude to her pissed me off. She'd been my PA since I opened. She worked hard and did everything I asked her to do.

"Who is this person?" I demanded. I couldn't begin to think who it could be.

"Wouldn't tell me his name. Just said he was an old friend and he wanted to see you. *Now.*" Winter widened her bright green eyes and grimaced.

I glanced at Georgie who looked concerned.

"How long has he been here?" I asked.

"Fifteen minutes tops. I told him you were busy. It got so bad I had to head down to see you. I'm sorry. I know how you hate being disturbed during a shoot."

"Don't worry about that. I'm sorry you had to deal with such an asshole."

Who the hell could it be? People knew not to rub me the wrong way. I wasn't sure who'd be brave enough to try, and in my own building. I pressed my lips together and looked back at Georgie.

"Georgie I'm sorry I'm just gonna go see who this is."

"By yourself? What if it's that idiot Tyson?" She

blinked several times and looked at me like I should have guessed right off the bat that it could be him.

Tyson and I dated for three months. That was just before I opened the fashion house. I didn't think it was him though for the simple fact that I knew too many of his secrets. The kind of secrets the soon-to-be state's attorney would absolutely not want unleashed.

Pretty certain that he didn't want the world knowing he was a pimp.

Yes, a damn pimp. Boy did I ever have my share of bad luck with men.

Tyson was right up there with the worst of the bunch. He was engaged now to a woman who looked like a Stepford wife, and lived like he had this clean life-style. Georgie must have thought it was him because when I left him the man wouldn't leave me alone. He went all stalker boy on me.

"I don't think Tyson would call himself my friend, and he wouldn't come here like that."

"I'm coming with you," Georgie insisted, walking ahead of me in the direction of my office.

I left Winter and caught up with Georgie.

"Georgie, I'll go in by myself," I maintained.

"No, nobody just goes into someone's office demanding to speak to them. It sounds weird." She gave me an incredulous stare.

I sighed agreeing with her.

God… what the hell awaited me? I was really hoping I'd just have a nice lunch with my friend and come back to finish up. I had so much to do. So much to organize for the damn show. I didn't want anything to go wrong.

We got up to my office and I noticed the door was ajar.

Assuming dragon bitch mode, I straightened up and pushed it open.

A tall, muscular man wearing a Boss suit stood by the wall of glass windows with his back to us. Tall and packing the kind of muscle you'd find on an athlete or a military man. The sun beamed down on his neatly-cut, spiky black hair picking out the lighter parts.

I opened my mouth to speak but the dragon bitch mode façade faded in an instant when he turned around to face me and I saw who he was.

The air left my lungs and I didn't quite know how or why I didn't collapse.

Bright, bright blue eyes bore into me like daggers, looking at me exactly the way I imagined he'd look after what I did.

What I did years ago.

His wide powerful shoulders tensed and his face hardened up straightaway at the sight of me, commanding attention to the perfect chisel in his jaw and the deep angles and planes God took his time to sculpt into his face.

His was a face I'd spent years committing to memory.

His was a face I saw in my dreams, and nightmares because he wasn't in my life anymore.

Friend... old friend...

No... he was so much more than that. He represented the past and all I'd left behind. He was supposed to be my future.

He was Ryan O'Shea.

Ryan O'Shea, the man who was my nightmare and savior. The man who was my first everything.

He was the man I was never to see again.

The man I was told to leave alone.

He was the man my heart sacrificed and I never thought I'd come face to face with him again.

I never planned to.

I hadn't seen him in seventeen years.

Why was he here now?

CHAPTER 2

Ryan

GREAT…

She was just looking at me.

Seventeen long years had passed and that was all she could do.

But then… what the fuck did I expect?

She was here in L.A. living the life I knew she wanted. Living the life she told me she dreamed of. In fact, she all but predicted everything she was now, and I noticed even more had come her way.

D'Angelo was a nice name. Great for her brand and

a great cover. Had to admit though that I preferred her real name, *Lana Connell*. Although I'd had plans to give her mine.

What a fool I was with that fantasy and what kind of fool was I to drop my guard and let her in?

I wished like fuck someone could have told me that the memory of her would plague me this whole time and the void she left would never be filled.

Now look at her.

I'd gotten on the plane this morning from Wilmington International full of wrath, ready to breathe fire. I was ready for war. Literally ready to destroy everything in my wake.

Yet... as I gazed at her I couldn't stop myself from remembering her the way I used to.

Nearly twenty years had passed, but she still looked like the Lana I knew.

Standing before me with her feet planted to the ground in her heels and the little summer dress that graced her body, the shock of seeing me might have robbed her of speech but she still looked every bit like the girl I'd loved.

Silence filled the space between us. Her standing paces away from me, both of us just staring at each other.

"*Ryan...*" she spoke my name, but I didn't answer.

There was so much I'd wanted to say. I just didn't know what to start with. It felt a little like the past when I used to watch her and think about what we could talk about.

I was the bully, an asshole of a guy who probably should have known better than to stick my nose where it didn't belong with a sweet girl like her.

Our maid's daughter.

Our maid, Amelia Connell, who was like a second mother to me. If I were honest, I'd have to admit that there were many instances where I'd felt her love exceeded that of my own mother.

Her daughter though... sweet as she was, there had to have been a side to her that had no compassion. Had to be to explain what she did, and how she crushed me.

I should have stayed away from her back then and I hated that I was still so drawn to her now, even after so long.

Her with that dark brown skin that looked bronze in the sunlight. Literally like golden metal with the hint of a shimmer that always sparkled. And her warm brown eyes that constantly held aspiration and hope, like she carried her dreams with her wherever she went.

As she shifted her weight from one foot to the next I could still see it. The sunlight beaming from the window caught her in all the right places, and enhanced the aspiration in her eyes and her beauty.

Seventeen years older looked good on her but I wasn't here for that. I'd flown across the country to see her face to face with one mission on my mind.

I was here to get information, and clarification.

"Lana are you okay?" Asked the woman beside her at the door.

It was only then that Lana blinked and turned to her.

"Yes... um... Georgie... can I call you later?" There was a tremor in her voice that I didn't miss.

"Are you sure?" Georgie asked, looking me over with deep curiosity. "I wouldn't like to leave you knowing you aren't safe." She continued to stare at me.

Ballsy. A little like Lana in the moments where she'd surprised me.

"I'm safe and fine... I'll call you later." Lana told her and with that the woman left and Lana closed the door.

She tucked a lock of her long black hair behind her ear and those bright brown eyes returned their focus to me. "Ryan... how did you find me?"

I balled my fist at my side and intensified my stare.

Maybe I expected her to say sorry she left the way she did. Without goodbye. Maybe I expected an explanation of *why* she left.

Not her asking me *how* I found her.

"It's not relevant, Lana *Connell*." She tensed when I said her old name. "That part is not relevant in the least. Fucking hell, you must have really wanted to stay hidden, changing your name and all. How come you kept the first name? Why not change it all?" My nostrils flared.

"Ryan... I ..."

I narrowed my eyes at her and decided that actually, I didn't want an explanation. I didn't want anything that didn't form part of why I was here.

"Save it." I dismissed her next words with a wave of my hand as her mouth opened like she was going to say something more. "I'm here to find out why you sent the police to my family to interrogate them on something that wasn't their fault."

Her eyes grew wide. *"What?"*

"The police are reinvestigating your mother's death. Clearly you must have sent them to us. What the fuck is that all about Lana? You couldn't leave well enough alone. You told me you thought her death was suspicious, I just never realized you were talking about my family. We cared for you. We treated you and your mother like family. How dare you do this to us?"

"I don't know what the hell you're talking about," she blurted, hands shaking. "I don't know what you're saying to me. I would never do that." A tear ran down her cheek.

While she looked like she was telling the truth, I didn't know if I could believe her. She'd looked to me like she was telling the truth too when she first told me she loved me and look how that turned out.

"I don't know you... I never did. And I'm just guessing that with your newfound cushy lifestyle you've just decided to hire the best people you can find to dig up a seventeen year old unsolved case. I get that you grieved for your mother. We all did. But this is shit. Absolute shit and you've made a big mistake coming for us with this bullshit."

"I didn't," she countered.

"Whatever. Whatever Lana. Just call off your hounds. My mother has cancer. She is a very sick woman and doesn't need this. You know I don't stand for any shit, and if I'm made to fight back I will and you won't like it."

"This is insane. I haven't done anything. I've been in Brazil for the last four weeks. I don't know who contacted the police but it wasn't me."

"Somebody did," I retorted, still not quite believing her. She didn't have to physically go to the police, with all the money she had I was certain she could have arranged something with someone.

I came from wealth so I knew how things worked. I knew money talked when you needed it to. I'd seen it many times in my life and career as an attorney. There wasn't anything money and power couldn't accomplish and Miss Lana here had grown up to be a very powerful woman.

"It wasn't me. You have to believe me. Ryan, that whole time was a very painful part of my life. It was the worst, and very difficult to move past, but I have. When I left Wilmington I closed that chapter of my life."

I wished like hell I didn't feel the sting her words dealt me. Like a blow to my heart.

But there…

That was the answer.

My father always told me the answer you were looking for wasn't always the one you wanted, or the one you wanted to hear. I always had the disadvantage of being stubborn. It made me hold on to stuff that I shouldn't. Memories I shouldn't.

Memories of her I shouldn't keep. Not a guy like me.

I nodded. "Yes, you did. You absolutely fucking did close that chapter of your life. It just would have been more humane to tell me you didn't want to be with me rather than leave the way you did. Would have been nice for me to also know that chapter was closed."

The vibrancy in her skin faded as I spoke. "I didn't mean that," she breathed.

I smirked without humor. I didn't know who the

fuck she was trying to fool. Not me. I was many years away from being the fool.

Looking away from her, I walked out of her office leaving her staring after me open mouthed.

This here was it. I'd close the chapter too.

I needed to.

You ask the girl you think you're in love with to run away with you, you plan it in every detail and even agree to go where she wants so she can go to college, you offer to pay for everything and take care of her. You think it's all in motion and while it might be crazy, it will work because you love each other.

Except she never showed up.

She never met me and since I'd refused to believe she'd just left like everyone else assumed I looked for her everywhere. *For years.*

I'd never allowed myself to get over her, not properly and I swear to God it was the way she'd left me bamboozled that accounted for the poor choices I made afterward.

She'd hurt me the most.

Finding out my five year old son wasn't mine didn't even hurt me as much as her departure.

Maybe that was because I was already broken.

Can't fix something that's already damaged.

My visit may have been a lost cause if the whole police thing wasn't her doing.

Whether it was or not, it was closure for me.

I'd said what I wanted to say.

I just wished it had made me feel better. Maybe that would come with time and I would forget her as easily as she'd forgotten me.

CHAPTER 3

LANA

OH GOD...

My breath caught in my throat. It caught right there and I couldn't breathe.

I had to rush over to the window and open it to let some fresh air in.

The whoosh of air that flowed in cascaded over me and soothed the tingle in my nerves. *But,* only a little.

I didn't think anything could truly calm me down.

Shit... that really was Ryan.

It was really him. Not a dream, not a figment of my imagination. It was him.

It was him and he'd just dropped a bomb on me about this reinvestigation.

What the fuck?

I suppose no one would have contacted me because I'd had my name changed by petition. It was my way of starting over after what happened.

I kept my first name because my father gave it to me. He named me Lana after my great grandmother, and I kept it in honor of him. He died in the Gulf War. I was only two years old and I didn't even know him, but the way Mama spoke about him kept him alive for me.

D'Angelo was a cool name I'd made up. It took me places and helped me to heal, but not forget.

I never forgot Ryan.

Never.

People said you never forgot your first love. It was true, and worse when your first love was your everything. It was soul crushing when you never had the life you thought you were going to have with them.

If only he knew the truth.

The truth of what happened was nothing like what I made it look like, and definitely not what he'd thought.

The truth was so awful that when I'd left Wilmington, it was never to return.

That was the plan until today.

The police were reinvestigating Mama's death.

Why?

What had they found?

She died seventeen years ago.

What could they have possibly found?

I had to find out what was happening. I needed to.

So that meant going back.

The door opened and I turned to see Georgie coming back in.

"I'm sorry. Call me the worrywart but ..." her voice trailed off when she saw my face and the tear drift down my cheek. "Jesus, Lana what happened? Are you okay?" She rushed over to me and took hold of my shoulders.

I shook my head. It was all I could do to answer.

"Talk to me Lana. Who was that guy?"

"Ryan... Ryan O'Shea." The minute I said that her eyes glazed with shock and her jaw dropped. She was the only person I'd ever told my story to.

"*Oh my God.*"

"Yeah." I moved my hand up to my head and exhaled a ragged breath.

"Lana... It's gonna be okay. I'm here." She pulled me into her arms for a reassuring hug. "Talk to me."

We pulled apart and I motioned for her to sit on the sofa by the bookcase.

We sat next to each other and I shuffled to face her, trying to combat the numbness that had taken me.

It was strange how not even twenty minutes ago, I

was consumed with my photoshoot and getting my work done.

Shit, I'd even been thinking of food and girl time with Georgie at Bob's Diner.

Now my stomach had twisted into so many knots that I didn't know if I could eat again, and my brain was scrambled.

"What happened with him?" Georgie asked.

I was momentarily stuck on how to proceed, still I willed myself to continue.

"He said the police are doing some kind of reinvestigation of my mother's death."

Her eyes clouded and her brows pinched. "They would only do that if they found something to reinvestigate."

"Yeah, but what? What could they have found? She killed herself." I brought my hands together to stop them from shaking and when she saw she reached over to take them into hers.

Saying it still didn't feel real. I still couldn't believe it. Mama jumped off a bridge and her body was found washed up on the riverbank. That's what happened. That's what the police said, except it never sounded like something my mother would do.

"Ryan said the police contacted his family. He thought I sent them. That's why he came to see me," I continued. "I don't know how he found me."

"He seemed to know exactly where to look. Lana, you've moved around a lot since and this place has only been set up for the last year."

"Yeah. I guess somehow he knew where to look."

Clearly he'd checked up on me. I'd looked in on him too. Not for long and not often. Just enough to know he was okay, and doing what he was meant to do. Then I willed myself to move on.

My shoulders slumped and I looked down at the marble floor, nearly getting lost in the swirly patterns. I brought my gaze back up to meet hers and pulled in a deep breath.

"I loved him... Georgie," I stated breathlessly and her eyes filled with deep sympathy.

"I know. I... know."

"He thinks I just left. He was so angry with me. It's hard to look at someone who used to love you and see hate in their eyes." What else could it look like with the way I'd departed? I was so stupid. I'd said that like I expected him to think something else. I'd never even had wishful thinking on my side.

"Maybe this is a way of telling him the truth." She actually looked hopeful.

I shook my head. There was no way I was doing that... "No... there's no point." The time had passed for that. "It's minor in the grand scheme of things."

"Well, I'm here for you, whatever you need. What-ever you decide."

"I have to go back, Georgie. I have to."

She nodded. "And I'm coming with you."

"No, you mustn't. Georgie you just got married. You can't leave Pat just like that, the man can barely stand to be without you for a day."

She chuckled. "He's going to have to be okay. You've always been there for me when I needed you. Now's my turn to be there for you. This isn't something you should handle on your own."

Well... I couldn't argue with that. I absolutely couldn't refute her words. Right now I wasn't sure how I'd get through the next minute, let alone make the arrangements to get myself to Wilmington.

"Thank you. Georgie... thank you. I never expected this to happen."

"I know. It feels very ominous to me. We don't know what instigated this reinvestigation." She raised her palms and lifted her shoulders.

I didn't... I had no idea what it might be and when Mama died I was beside myself with grief. The world turned every which way except the way it should have.

Georgie tapped my knuckles and gave me a little smile. "Here's what we're gonna do. I'll go grab us some lunch and we'll plan out our travel and make all the arrangements we need."

29

I took her hand, now grateful for her assistance. "Thank you for being here, and staying back. I would have fallen apart on my own."

"You know you're welcome." She stood to go. "I'll be back as quickly as possible, but call me if you need me."

"Thanks."

I watched her leave and as soon as the door closed my shoulders tensed with the weight of the situation. And memories.

The memories were always something I'd never been able to deal with.

I saw Ryan O'Shea today. I still couldn't believe it.

Ryan.

My Ryan.

No.

He wasn't mine anymore, hadn't been in seventeen years.

How could it have been so long?

I actually saw him today.

There was so much in his words that showed what he must have thought about me.

The tears I'd been holding back rolled down my cheeks and I gripped the edge of the sofa as if it could keep me from falling apart.

I gazed outside the window. As a light drizzle started to fall from the sky it reminded me of the day

I'd left Wilmington. It was drizzling just like it was now.

Ryan hated me for leaving and he was right to. Everything he'd said in regards to the way I left was completely correct. Except at the time I wasn't really given a choice when his beloved mother threw me out and threatened to destroy me if I didn't stay away from her son.

That was what happened.

Kathy O'Shea told me to go. She told me to leave Ryan, get out of his life and stay away from him. She'd stopped me from meeting him.

I squeezed my eyes shut at the memory, willing it all to go away. However, the sting of her viperous tongue, came rushing back on me and it could have been happening right now.

In my mind I could see Kathy with her perfect blonde up do, bright red lips pursed together and a heavy scowl of distaste on her face along with pleasure from my reaction when she'd asked me if I thought I was good enough for her son.

Then she followed that up by telling me Ryan could and should do better, and if I loved him I'd leave so he could make better choices with his life.

Her tirade continued to inform me that I was the maid's daughter and she didn't want her son associating himself with the help.

The way she'd glowered at me as she told me Ryan needed to be with a girl of his own league left no doubt in my mind that it wasn't just the fact that I was the help's daughter that irked her. She also didn't want him with me because I was black.

Having someone talk to you like that at eighteen years old was truly awful.

It was so much worse when you'd just lost everything. I'd buried my mother two months before and I was a mess.

I was a complete mess. My mind fragile and my heart shattered from the loss.

Over the time I'd known her Mrs. O'Shea had always been cold toward me and Mama, but she never truly expressed her pure dislike until that day.

I knew she didn't like either of us, and worst because Mr. O'Shea did. He treated us like we were part of the family. She truly hated that and indicated it, just never outrightly said it.

It might have made it easier though if she'd shown her true colors before. It would have given me a heads up that she was actually evil.

Ryan and I were seeing each other in secret. We were supposed to leave for New York and she stepped in. Kathy O'Shea stepped in big time, intercepted, and well and truly put me in my place. When I told her I was in love with him and wanted the best for him it enraged her. The woman threw me out of her house herself, and that was when she threatened to destroy me.

I didn't know what she meant by destroy, but I didn't need to ask.

The thing was... it wasn't that part that made me leave.

It was the worry of not being good enough for Ryan. It was clear I had nothing to offer him and he was giving up a lot to be with me.

I reached across the coffee table and grabbed a few tissues from the Kleenex box to dry my eyes.

Ryan might have been a rebel, but the guy was practically a genius with an IQ that was through the roof. I didn't know anybody else who hated college as much as he did, and just turned up for their first batch of legal exams and aced them without a day of study. He'd said the answers he gave were logical and made sense.

He'd wanted to become an artist and that was what he was going to do in New York, while I went to design school. He was a fantastic artist but with his family business being law, he would have worked wonders. That was supposed to be the plan his parents thought he'd follow.

I wasn't his problem to deal with. That's what Kathy O'Shea said and I agreed.

She thought I would have just been using him for his money, a means to an end as I'd lost my mother.

I'd told myself that leaving him would allow him to be who he was supposed to be. So I left, leaving behind the boy I'd loved and the memory of my mother.

It made sense for Georgie to suggest telling Ryan the truth. It did. Especially seeing the state I was clearly in.

Many years ago, after I finished college, I nearly did find him to tell him what happened. But I'd stopped myself after I'd called his father's law firm and was told he worked there.

That told me he'd made it.

It told me he was doing what he was supposed to be doing.

He was where he was supposed to be and it was right for me to have left.

The truth wouldn't help anybody now, and not when Kathy had cancer.

When I'd dropped the comment that Mama's suicide was suspicious, I didn't actually aim it at anyone. It was suspicious because it simply was.

I was about to find out why.

I was about to go back to the past I'd run from.

Seeing Ryan today was something I never expected.

The memories and his presence took me right back

to the moment things changed between us. It was like something unlocked.

Like truth was speaking and had allowed the walls of everything else to fade

so we could see there was more to us than met the eye. More than we even knew.

He was the bully I should have stayed away from.

I wished I had.

My shoulders wracked as I started to sob, crying tears that poured from my weeping soul.

CHAPTER 4

LANA

NINETEEN YEARS AGO ...

A series of laughter sounded behind my back. I turned and glared knowing it would mean nothing but I still did it anyway.

It was my way of retaliating. Even if all I could do was look and glower, I would do it.

The smell of tuna in my locker was overpowering, suggesting it had been in there from either last night or yesterday.

As the odor wafted out, the students passing by covered their noses. Some started laughing.

"Hey Connell, you stink!" cried Mort Peterson, the captain of the basketball team. His girlfriend Carolina started to laugh and the laughter continued with the bunch of hyenas who were responsible.

The main hyena laughed the loudest. It would have been his idea to do this to me, just like all the other shit he'd done to me since Mama and I went to live with him and his family eight years ago.

Mama had a live in maid position at the O'Shea mansion. For me it was like living in hell.

In fact, I felt certain that the devil might have had more compassion than him.

His father would have told him off, his mother was quiet. She always gave me the creeps with her cold calculating eyes. Always watching and observing. Never really saying much. She was the kind of woman who would give a disapproving glare and it would be enough to warn you.

I was sure though that Ryan O'Shea didn't care one way or the other, because he had his parents wrapped around his thumb most of the time. Just not when it came to sneaking girls in the house.

He was doing this to me because apparently it was my fault his father caught Tiffany Tate in his room giving him a blow job.

My fault because I told his father I couldn't get inside his room to clean it. Mama had to go to the dentist so I filled in for her afternoon work.

How the hell was I supposed to know Ryan was in the room with that skank and he'd locked the door from the inside. His father used a master key and found them. *We* found them.

My fault.

It was apparently my fault too that his father had punished him by taking away his motorcycle and the new convertible.

Poor Ryan… *boohoo.* How so, so very unfortunate for him that he had to use last year's Porsche at the start of his senior year, and all the other jocks and snobbish assholes had the latest.

Ugh, I hated living with him, and it was worse that I felt so stupid for feeling jealous.

Me jealous over the skank with the guy who treated me like shit. The said guy my very, very stupid heart warmed to whenever he was near me.

What the hell was wrong with me?

I was sixteen years old and had no form of sexual experience at all. I'd never even kissed a boy but I wasn't stupid. I knew what she was doing to him and I actually felt jealous of the fact that she was the kind of girl Ryan went for.

The head cheerleader on the squad. The most

popular girl at school who was of course beautiful and well loved by everyone. And yes rich, just like him.

Tiffany was on his arm now, laughing at me while I had to deal with the damn tuna in my locker. Freaking fantastic.

He glanced over at me and gave me the habitual sneer so I looked away, took the tuna out, and left the stupid locker open to air out.

I felt for certain this would be the first strike. Tomorrow was Mrs. O'Shea's dinner party where I was sure he'd deal more torture to me.

I was wrong…

Before the day was out, I had one of my math books stolen and when I found it, all the pages were glued together. But my personal favorite was the petrified rat I found in my gym bag. The thing looked like it had been dead for weeks. Knowing Ryan, he'd probably found it and kept it specially for me.

This was what my life was like.

He was seventeen about to turn eighteen and in the year above me, he'd be going to college next year. I didn't think it was insane for me to wonder why he thought he could act like such a brat with his childish pranks.

And I just had to take it.

Why?

Because Mama wanted to keep the peace. The

Donovans paid her well, we got to live in a nice house for free, and she wanted to make sure she could save up to send me to college. She wanted to make sure she had enough to give me all that I wanted.

While I loved the thinking behind that, a majority of the time I truly wished she could do something else for work and I would happily take living in a box rather than being there in the O'Shea mansion.

I was definitely going away to college and counting down the days even though I had a little under two years before I went.

We'd been here for so long and year in, year out was the same.

The O'Sheas did pay Mama well and we would have had enough money for everything if my aunt wasn't always in trouble and needing money to bail her out.

I knew Aunt Larissa was a drug addict, my cousin told me and by the same token I knew that Mama always being there to help her when she needed it wasn't helping her. The only thing it was doing was robbing us of a better life.

Robbing *me* of a better life.

I stayed in the safety of my room for the whole morning the next day.

Usually on Saturday, I'd go to the library first thing at the community center to swim, but it was safer to stay in because I knew Ryan was just waiting for me to come out. I knew later on was going to be awful so I just wanted a quiet morning with my fashion magazines and design books. There was a skirt I wanted to make. I'd saved up to buy the cloth two weeks ago and the stones to put on it. I was going for a Boho chic look I'd seen a lot in the spring. Most designers were doing their collections with that in mind.

That was what I wanted to be. A fashion designer. I was going to college to study that. I was hoping to get into Parsons in New York. That was where I had my heart set. I tried not to think of it too much because realistically it was years away and seriously expensive.

Until that time though, I thought I could do what I loved. That meant making my own inspired designs on days like Saturday where I had a few spare hours.

I emerged just before the party started so I could help Mama. I'd managed to do some drawings for the pattern I'd follow for my skirt and created a little motif with the diamantes.

The plan was to do what was needed then get back up to my room and start sewing. I currently sewed by hand. The next round of savings would hopefully get me a sewing machine.

I went downstairs through the back hallway and

found Mama in the kitchen with the kitchen staff. She already looked rushed off her feet.

"Good sweetie, you're down," she said, smiling at me. "Can you start serving the canapes? The guests have already started to arrive."

"Sure." I returned the smile. Anything for her, although I did wonder who'd be here at this time. Who got to a party this early?

I got the answer when I took the tray of canapes out to the poolside and saw Ryan and friends. Friends as in his stupid jerk football friends Tom, Paul, Carson, and Barney.

Barney, I didn't know who could have a name like that and automatically think they were cool. No riches on earth could make that name cool, yet when this guy saw me, he wrinkled his nose like he'd just smelled something bad and looked at me like he'd stepped in shit.

"Maid girl." He called out to me.

I didn't answer. I did not speak to him or any of them for that matter.

I just walked up to the little buffet table and set down the tray. The asshole however thought it would be a good idea to come up to me and snap his fingers in front of my face.

His long blond hair was a matted mess today and his ice blue glacier-like eyes gave me an arctic stare.

"I'm talking to you," he said in a harsh tone. When I didn't answer and continued to glower at him the group started to laugh. "Oh she doesn't speak. Something wrong with you?" He stepped closer, and closer and made the mistake of stepping in my personal space with that stupid finger-snapping shit in my face.

How I hated that. Talk to me badly, tease me even, but fingers snapping right in my face, as in an inch from my nose, was a hell no.

I shocked him by stepping forwards in a swift move and holding my hand up in front of him.

"Don't do that," I told him through gritted teeth. "And I'm not your maid, nor your girl so don't speak to me."

I may have sounded ballsy like I could take care of myself and maybe it would have worked on a different group. For these guys though, no, not so much. He just laughed, as did the others.

My gaze snapped to Ryan who to my surprise was just sitting on the deck chair watching me. This behavior from his friends was because of him. Head bully. He made them think it was okay to treat people the way they did.

A series of giggles cut into my glare at him and I looked to the top of the stairs to see the girls arriving. The bitch Tiffany spotted me and whispered something to her friend.

That was my cue to leave, so I did.

With the canapes delivered, I felt I could buy some time doing something else.

I went back to the kitchen and saw Mama making a pitcher of fruit punch.

"Sweetie can you go ask Ryan and his friends if they want some drinks? Mr. O'Shea wants me to make sure they have enough mocktails so they don't sneak away the alcohol." She chuckled.

My heart dropped into my stomach. "Can I do something else? Please?"

Maybe it was the defeat in my eyes and the withered expression on my face but she seemed to take note.

"Lana, what's up? You've been in your room all day, now you've come down and you look like you'd rather be somewhere else."

I glanced at Chef Moore and he raised his brows. It was funny everyone else seemed to see what was going on, except her.

"I would, I don't want to go back outside with them. Mama, if I breathe the wrong way they all make fun of me." I knew I sounded like a whiner but it was the truth.

"Oh sweetie they don't mean anything by it. Come on help me out here. I need you. I want this part done so we can start on the food. The main guests will arrive soon." She gave me a little pat on my back. "Come on sweetie. Remember every time you pout you encourage a wrinkle." Mama loved Marilyn Monroe and often quoted her.

"That's not true, wrinkles just happen to come when they feel like," I countered.

"Nope, I'm saving you. Trust me. Plus, how will you look on stage at the grand opening of your fashion show in a few years' time with wrinkles when you're only twenty something." She giggled. "Imagine all your guests including me, wearing their finest get up, looking on at you. A girl has to be the queen of her own show."

That made me smile. She always knew how to reach me. Somehow she'd say just the right thing to melt me like butter.

My own show. I would be happy to work for a big designer, but my own line of clothes in a fashion show was the stuff dreams were made of.

"Oh Mama." I grinned, slumping my shoulders.

"Don't you oh Mama me, sweet girl. I'm being serious. I'll be the proud mother of the acclaimed fashion designer. Of course I'll have my hair done and make you proud too." she gave the flicks of her hair a little tap and the ends bounced. When she did that she always reminded me of someone classy like Billie Holliday. But Mama wore her shoulder length hair like Marilyn Monroe and had her figure too. Along with the winning smile she could get anybody to do anything.

"You win." I sighed with a little laugh when Mama gave me what she called her Marylyn wink.

"Of course. Make a girl laugh and you can get her to do anything."

Both Chef Moore and his assistant chuckled.

Putting on a brave face, I made my way back outside and that was where my disastrous evening really kicked off.

Because I'd told Barney not to speak to me or call me Maid Girl, the group did it even more and laughed.

What was worse was watching Ryan get friendly with Tiffany's tongue. At one point I had to wonder if they were doing a thorough check of each other's tonsils.

It rubbed me the wrong way that I took such great note of anything he did like that and no matter what I did to ignore my stupid reaction, I'd just end up feeling worse.

Today I was more inclined to agree with Barney. Maybe something was wrong with me. How else would I explain my fascination with a guy who'd bullied me since I was eight.

I got a break from it all when Mama asked me to start cleaning the toilets and bathrooms upstairs. It was a most welcomed break because there were two bathrooms and three toilets up there. I'd worked out that if I started with the larger bathroom first I could spend a whole hour there cleaning all the tiles and the windows.

The guests would be using the downstairs facilities so I would basically be left alone, and that would be my evening sorted out.

It was after ten when I finished and headed to my room.

When I got to the corner of the corridor, voices filtered out.

"What is she doing with this?" Someone asked. It sounded like one of Tiffany's bitch friends. "Where the hell would she even be wearing something like this?" She laughed.

"It's the new toilet look. Got to dress right to clean shit." That was Tiffany and she was in my room.

I rushed to the door to see her and Marsha inside. They had my stuff. My fabric and diamantes.

"What are you doing in here?" I demanded. "This is my room."

Tiffany narrowed her eyes at me. "*Yours?* I wasn't aware that anything in this house belonged to you."

"That is my personal property, put it down."

"Is she supposed to be rude?" Marsha asked.

"No," Tiffany answered in that snooty manner I hated. "She's a servant, she isn't supposed to be anything or do anything unless she's told." She tossed her platinum blond hair over her shoulder and stared me down.

What a bitch. What a fucking bitch.

"Give me my stuff back," I demanded, putting my hand out. She was holding my silk cloth and Marsha had the pack of diamantes.

"Didn't say please," Marsha teased. "Maybe you should try using the word."

"I will do nothing of the sort. You're in my room with my stuff, give it back."

Tiffany stepped up to me. "I wonder where does a girl like you get money to buy stuff like this? Did you steal it? Maybe from Ryan's mom?"

"Give me my stuff back!" I cried. The whole horridness of the situation got to me. Tears stung the backs of my eyes and I just wished they'd give me my things and leave me alone. "Give it back."

"Here," Marsha said but she opened the box of diamantes and threw them all over the room.

"No, stop it." I moved to her to stop her from dashing away the rest. I'd gotten just enough to put on the skirt and they would be a mission to find.

She threw the box through the window and started laughing along with Tiffany.

"Why do you guys have to be such jerks?" I cried.

"You haven't seen anything yet," Tiffany answered and showed me what a bitch she could be when she held up the material and ripped it down the middle.

I lunged for her to stop her from doing further damage but Marsha held me back, grabbing my arms to keep me in place. She was taller than me and stronger so I was helpless.

My heart broke when Tiffany grabbed the scissors from the dressing table and started cutting up the beautiful silk fabric I'd saved up for, *for weeks*, into tiny pieces. She cut it all up and dashed it on the floor. It was only once the damage was done that Marsha released me. All that bravado I'd previously exhibited was gone and tears streamed down my cheeks. I crumbled to the floor with the material, crying.

"Pick that up *Maid Girl*," Tiffany taunted. "Maybe you can –"

Her voice cut when someone cleared their throat at the door. I didn't bother to look to see who it was. No one here was on my side so it could only be another one of them from the group.

"What's going on in here?" It was Ryan.

"We were just messing around." Tiffany laughed.

I glanced over my shoulder and noted the stern look on his face.

"This area is off limits, go back downstairs," he ordered.

"Ryan come on –"

"Get out!" he barked.

I'd only ever heard him sound like that out on the football field. It was a tone that told you not to mess with him, or make him repeat himself.

It was also the sort of commanding tone to make you listen and do as you were told, which was what the girls did.

They left.

I really wished I could stop the tears but the truth was I'd had enough. I'd had enough and was ready to walk. Leave and go anywhere that wasn't here.

Aunt Larissa dropped out of school when she was sixteen and I knew people who did it. I didn't know what would happen to me if I left school and just left this God forsaken house but surely anything was better than this.

I looked down at the shreds of cloth scattered on the floor and covered my mouth to hold back the fresh bout of tears that came.

I'd expected Ryan to leave with them but he didn't. He was still standing there and I was waiting for him to say whatever he wanted to say to me. More punishment for the other day.

However, he kept his silence.

He kept his silence, walked around to face me then crouched down. When he started picking up the shreds of material I narrowed my eyes at him.

"What the hell's this for?" He picked up the pieces and allowed them to drift back down to the ground.

I had half a mind to ignore him but I knew that would only end up being to my detriment. The same thing that barely worked on the friends wouldn't work with him. Plus, it was different when it came to him since this was his house.

"I sew... I make clothes," I answered in a meek voice.

"Since when?" He prodded and those bright blue eyes that enchanted me from day one bored into mine.

"Always."

He held my gaze, then looked at the material and diamantes over the ground. I geared myself up for some sort of sarcasm but he said nothing.

Instead he surprised me by grabbing the wastepaper bin and gathering the shreds of material from the ground to toss inside. He gathered the whole bunch and left.

With him gone I sank back against the wall and cried myself to sleep right there.

When I woke the next day there was a bag next to me. One of those couture looking bags I'd seen Mrs. O'Shea with.

I straightened, wondering where it came from. Usually me looking in bags resulted in seeing something that terrified me.

When I peeked inside the bag I didn't know whether to scream or cry.

I reached in and pulled out what looked like yards of silk fabric the same cerise color as what was destroyed last night. Inside too was a big bag of diamantes.

One hell of a size I would never have been able to afford and it was the good stuff.

It all brought a smile to my face but damn, as I thought of who could have bought it for me my heart squeezed. The only person who'd have the heart to do something so nice for me was Mama.

But... the only person who had the means to do this for me and knew I needed it was the guy I thought had no heart.

Or... maybe he did.

I got dressed and went outside to the garage. On Sundays he would always be out here working on one of his cars, or his bike.

There he was.

He was in the garage working on one of his old cars.

Looking amazing as always, with that bad boy image he was so good at. A cigarette was tucked behind his ear as he looked under the hood of his car. He wore a white t-shirt that clung to his muscles and Levi's that hung low on his hips.

Ryan looked up when I approached and stared at me, giving me that flat expressionless gaze.

I looked back in curiosity.

He wasn't known for doing anything nice, and not to me. What could have changed?

"What do you want?" he asked.

I wouldn't have normally gone any closer than I had but I did. I walked right up to him.

"Thank you," I told him.

The corners of his mouth lifted in that sexy half smile that made him look more alluring and the vision was enhanced when he tilted his head to the side and a lock of his slick black hair fell over his eye.

"What for?" he asked.

"The material and stones," I said pointedly.

"What if it wasn't me who got them for you? You just assume it was me?"

"It was you," I answered and he straightened up.

"What are you making?" he asked with narrowed eyes.

"A skirt."

"Where are you wearing the skirt?"

What an odd question. "Out."

His gaze hardened and when he stepped forwards I stepped backward. He did it again and so did I. The wall prevented me from going further. He sneered and blocked me in by placing his palms either side of me on the wall.

Then he moved closer until he was inches away

from my face. So close his warm breath tickled my nose.

"Out …with who?" he demanded.

I widened my eyes at him, looking at him in complete disbelief.

"No one, I told you I make clothes."

His gaze lowered to my top. It was a little camisole top I'd made last summer. I liked the way it fit me. My lips parted when he lifted the hem and tugged on the ends.

"You make this?" It was the way he was looking at me - something darkened in his eyes, darkened with desire and my breath hitched when the tips of his fingers brushed over the bare skin of my stomach.

"Yes," I breathed.

Instead of the flutter against my skin he pressed his finger into me, all the while holding my gaze.

The emotion that coursed through me awakened my senses, and sense of awareness. I didn't know what alternate dimension I'd just walked into but this couldn't be my reality.

Closer… he came closer and I almost thought he was going to kiss me. I almost felt his lips on mine.

Almost, and never.

The kiss was a breath away but he leaned near to my ear, slightly brushing against my cheek.

"It's nice," he whispered and I forgot what he was talking about.

I only remembered when he released the hold he had on the top and moved back, away from me.

Feeling momentarily stunned I wasn't sure what to do, so I moved to leave.

"Lana." He called after me.

I stopped and turned back to face him. "Yes."

"Make sure you show me this skirt of yours when it's done."

I raised my brows. "You want to see it?"

"Want to see you wearing it." He gave me a devilishly handsome smile.

"Okay," I replied and it felt like the first time we truly connected.

Something changed and I wasn't sure what it was, but it was something that piqued my interest.

CHAPTER 5

RYAN

PRESENT DAY...

I hated sleeping on the plane and going into work
straight after a flight.

Today it was a necessity. I had back to back meetings from nine o'clock and I needed to speak to Dad
about what was going on with the police.

It was him they'd contacted first to set up a meeting
to talk to the family.

That was two days ago.

Only two days ago, and it kick started my wrath.

We weren't really given much information, just contacted by Detective Gracen. I'd gone to the house to visit and got hit with the news. News that sent Mom to her bed. She was already frail as it was after that last round of chemo a few months back. That last round did her in, weakened her immensely. It was scary because I truly thought it would take her from me.

The sight of her frail appearance was what made me get on that plane.

After a busy morning I made my way to Dad's office at lunch time.

He was sitting behind his desk looking haggard and drained with dark circles under his eyes like he hadn't slept in weeks. Days ago when we got the news he seemed more in control, but maybe it was his worry over Mom that gave him this presence.

"Hey Dad," I said as I walked in.

"Hey kid," he breathed. He still called me kid, and still tried to keep up that positive appearance he'd always sported even when he was troubled.

I sat in the chair before him.

He'd been in meetings too since I got in. His schedule was crazier than mine. I had a lot of little things going on with different cases, but he had a big tradesmark dispute case that had gone on for months.

We both specialized in the same areas of law

because he wanted to keep the management of the business in the family. So while we had a few other attorneys working for us, we were the senior partners. Me being as specialized as him helped when Mom got sick.

"You okay?" I asked.

He released a heavy sigh and sat forward, resting his hands on the surface of his mahogany table.

"No. I'm not okay, kid." He shook his head. That answer there was the opposite of what he'd usually say. He'd sooner tell me he had things in hand than admit to not being okay. "I think I need to get Johnson to finish up the work on this case."

I frowned. Johnson was good at what he did but he always expected far too much in return, like we should be grateful or like he was doing us a favor. He was already on a higher salary than all the other attorneys and he was a junior associate. He just happened to have the expertise we needed for the more difficult intellectual property cases.

Dad considering enlisting Johnson's help also showed the situation was serious. He would never get anyone to help him or finish up his work if he didn't think it called for it.

"Ryan, don't give me that face. I'm going to need help so Johnson is it. If he's running the show on this case I won't have to worry."

"I get it. I'm just pissed because it's come to this." I

was more than pissed and still in two minds about whether or not it was Lana who'd contacted the police. I didn't want to look like a prick who didn't care or understand why she did it if it was her, but I saw what it did to Mom.

"Ryan, you shouldn't be pissed about that. I... also know you practically breezed down to L.A. yesterday, and I know you saw Lana."

I tensed. I didn't know how he knew but it wasn't difficult to figure out. For a start he knew I found her six years ago in L.A.

He knew because I'd told him. But what I never told him was the back story. However, my father was my father and didn't need to be told all that much to figure anything out. He could look at me and tell.

The same way he looked at me two days ago when he told me the police wanted to reinvestigate Amelia's death and in the same breath warned me away from seeing Lana. He'd just known what I was thinking.

"Dad, it's suspicious and completely out of the blue. It's clear to me that someone requested the reinvestigation."

"It wasn't her," he answered pointedly and I straightened up. "Had you stayed you would have known that. But... I guess you needed an excuse."

He intensified his stare and I felt like a child again,

the same boy who couldn't hide anything from his father.

Like my art when I was twelve. I tried to hide it because painting was so out of character for me. Him finding out about that was the first time I realized I couldn't hide anything from him.

Rebellious and wild as I was, he knew, always knew what I was up to even before I did it.

"Excuse?" I could still be stubborn and hold my own.

He held out his palms. "Sometimes it's what you don't say that speaks louder than words. Six years ago you told me you saw her in LA. I saw you sitting by the pond at the mansion just staring into space like someone died. When I asked what was wrong with you, you said you saw her and she was fine, designing her clothes. That was it...no elaboration. Just enough for me to deduce that she made it to where she wanted to be. I sat with you for an hour in silence and I only left when I realized you were so cut up that you couldn't talk. You couldn't talk and haven't said anything about her since. I'm still here if you need me, but know this, I am a hundred per cent cooperating with this investigation."

I didn't want to talk about Lana. Not to anyone, although the best person to speak to was Dad.

I just wanted to forget and maybe yesterday was the first step in doing so and truly moving on because I got the chance to give her the tamer version of a piece of my mind.

"What happened yesterday?" I asked bringing back the conversation to what we should be focusing on.

"I went to the station and spoke with the captain. He said there's some new evidence that's come to light. So the police just want to speak to us about it. Amelia lived with us. We were the closest people to her." He glanced down at the table and ran his hand over his beard when he looked back to me.

He'd always had the same look when the subject of Amelia came up. It was sad and it was like he'd lost something.

I'd been going through the shit I was going through at the time with college and I just wanted to leave everyone. Take my girl and go.

Even I noticed however that after Amelia's death, Dad wasn't the same.

"It's just a matter of formality," he added. "New evidence they need to investigate."

"Like what?" I had to know.

"It's a missing part of the autopsy report that was found."

I bit the inside of my lip. That did not sound good. I'd been in the legal world far too long to take something like that as anything besides serious.

"Dad, you can't sit there and tell me you think this is

just a matter of formality." Now I wished I'd stayed, I would have most likely gone with Dad to the station, and gotten this info. I would have looked into it a little more because it sounded even more serious than I'd previously thought.

Maybe though... I was really looking for an excuse to see Lana.

"I know, but I'm just going with what they said. Ryan, Amelia was such a happy person. There was no real inkling of whatever caused her to take her life. None. There one day with that good natured every-thing. Then gone the next day." He stopped and sadness filled his eyes.

It was a sadness that was still very much alive in me. "It still grieves me, Dad."

He bowed his head as if to show reverence and ran a hand over his salt and pepper beard. "I can't lie and tell you that her death didn't surprise me. When people take their lives the one's left behind are always wondering what they could have done differently. What they could have done more to stop it, or even help. It makes you wonder how she could have been so close and no one saw her pain."

I shook my head. "That's just the thing Dad, we didn't. She seemed fine the last time I saw her."

I was in the middle of finishing up the last semester of my first year at Georgetown. It was supposed to be my last. I went home for the weekend. It looked like I'd just gone back because I wanted to see my family, but really I'd missed my girl. I got home and saw Amelia in the garden, with Lana curled up at her feet listening to her read her poems. They'd caught me staring. I liked watching them together. It didn't matter how old Lana got, she always listened to her mother read.

"Maybe so." Dad's voice cut into the memory. "It doesn't make me wish any less that I could have saved her. She was good to us. She was good to me and the only thing I could have done for her is take care of her daughter, but as we know, Lana left. I looked for her too Ryan. Not for the years you looked but I looked for her."

"I know." He had. Dad looked for her for over a year and decided to call off the search party. He'd thought if she wanted to come home she would, and that we'd find her when she was ready to be found.

It made sense and realistically he couldn't be expected to look for her forever, nevertheless it didn't help me much.

"I looked for Lana everywhere I could and never found her. I would have taken care of her, because we were all she had left." His eyes glazed over with a sheen of purpose. "Ryan, I'm going to be honest with you. You and I both know the police wouldn't investigate if they didn't need to. Missing documents are like gold dust to us with our criminal law cases. You know it's something that could change the outcome of a scenario, or situation, a result. We were told Amelia committed suicide. If something different happened to her, or if there's something more that happened, I want to know. I want to know if there was more at work to her death."

He nodded and there was something in the depth of his light brown eyes that reached out to me. "I would greatly appreciate if you cooperated too and it maybe best to just leave Lana alone. Leave her out of this. I don't want to make things worse than they are, or have been. We don't know her reasons for leaving, disappearing more like. All I can assume is it must have been grief for her mother's death."

"Okay," I answered and it felt like the hardest thing in the world to say. I had no plans to see Lana. I could only imagine that she'd probably make contact with the police herself and that would be it. None of us needed to contact her for anything. I didn't. "What now?"

"I'm meeting with Detective Gracen tomorrow. He'll be questioning me."

"*Questioning*? That sounds like you need legal representation." I narrowed my eyes at him wondering if he was being serious, acting so cool and calm.

"I do not. Calm yourself Ryan."

"What am I supposed to do?"

"I imagine they will want to see you at some point

too. They want to question everyone and literally do a full reinvestigation. Recheck things out."

Mom wasn't going to like that. But as Dad said, matter of formality. I'd cooperate too. It was the least I could do for Amelia's sake, I just didn't like the vagueness and all the emotions it dug up.

"Fine, just let me know if you need me for anything else."

He looked me over and templed his fingers. "You haven't acted out the way you did days ago in years."

"What do you mean?" I sighed.

"You reminded me of you at nineteen when you wanted to drop out of college. I was shocked you didn't do it."

I didn't do it because plans changed up completely when Lana left. That part of me that found the strength to leave all the shit behind faded into the ether and I just stuck with what I was doing, settling for the life that had been paved out for me.

It changed me.

"Well, aren't you glad I stayed? We've worked wonders with the business." We had. O'Sheas LLP on Main Street turned into a chain of five multi-specialty law firms. The headquarters here in Wilmington along with another in Charlotte, then branches in New York, Chicago and Philadelphia. There was talk of expanding to LA and San Francisco.

That was what happened when Dad and I worked together.

"Money means nothing when you aren't happy." A sympathetic smile arched his lips. "We can work hard and achieve all manner of successes like we have, but I remember there was a time in my son's life when he was happy."

"Dad, I'm fine," I insisted.

He drew his brows together. "You say that, but the words don't feel true. The son I remember looked like he had a reason to live. Then things changed and he became a shell."

I pressed my lips together and tried to look like his words had no effect. "A shell Dad?"

"A shell. Not that I'm not thrilled with the success we've had, but I would have gladly kept on going with my one law firm that was making me wealthy, over the billion dollar fortune we have now, to see you the way you used to be." Dad nodded. "My artist."

I just stared at him.

He was always like that; even told me I had the choice of doing something else or working with him. That something else would have been art.

Mom was the one with the problem however, and I was a sucker for my mother. A big softie who would never defy his mother's wishes.

She'd wanted me to have the wealth of a lawyer, the

same kind Dad had. She thought it was a waste of my brain to do anything else.

"Well, things turned out the way they should," I pointed out.

"Did they?" He quirked a brow. "You never said how she was. Lana. Was she okay?"

Dad didn't know half of what I knew, and I knew more than I should. I simply nodded.

"She doing what she always wanted to do. Has her own brand now. Lana *D'Angelo.*" That was the first time I'd given him the surname.

"Lana *D'Angelo.*" He gave me a little smile, showing he was proud. At the same time, I could see the flicker of hurt in his eyes from how he'd worried about her.

"Lana *D'Angelo,*" I confirmed. She'd made it without me.

That was perhaps how it was supposed to be.

Dad smiled. "Must have been a shock to see you."

I didn't want to talk about it. I really didn't six years ago as much as I knew he would have wanted me to say more than I had, and I didn't want to talk now. Shutting down and shutting out was how I coped.

The result was it pushed everyone away, nevertheless it was what I needed.

"It was a shock."

"Is that it, nothing more you want to talk about?"

"No." My phone buzzed in my back pocket and as I

pulled it out the reminder of how much my life sucked stared me in the face.

It was Tiffany and I wasn't going to answer.

I wished like hell she'd just stop calling me, stop with everything.

Especially when Jack was with his grandparents.

I had no reason to speak to her other than about our son... well...*her son*, my child that I considered mine.

We'd been divorced now for eight months and just because I was talking to her on a cordial level didn't mean I was ready to jump in bed with her, like she thought. She'd shared our bed with half the town so I was sure some poor idiot would keep her company.

I stood up to go and Dad looked worried as he heard the phone ring out.

"Dad, I'll see you tomorrow. Let me know if I can do anything."

"Yeah ... sure." He nodded.

I was going back to work. Better to work than stick my nose back in reality.

Everything was so depressing and unbearable.

As the phone buzzed in my pocket again, I thought of Lana.

I ended whatever I had with Tiffany when I was eighteen to be with Lana and it actually felt like freedom.

How ironic it was that I'd ended up marrying

Tiffany and done everything I never wanted to do.

It was as if someone had shown me a version of my life. Of what would have happened if I'd chosen the alternate. Dad was right about me being a shell.

It was exactly what I felt like.

A shell. A shell and a shadow of my former self.

I drove home after work with everything on my mind. I hated having so much to think about. Seeing Lana again just added to it.

Before I even turned the corner for my house a sleek black Porsche came into view, parked on the drive.

My house was near the beach but in the crook between the woods and the estuary. Cape Fear River flowed into it bringing the scenery to life. I bought the place for the view.

I didn't recognize the car, but I didn't need to wonder who it belonged to for too long.

A woman with long black hair stood out in the distance by the boardwalk. Her hair drifted lightly in the breeze. Her beautiful dark skin looked striking against the white summer dress she wore and in the scenery before me with the oncoming evening she looked like a painting.

I'd imagined this happening so many times and called myself crazy for conjuring it that I had to wonder if my mind was screwing with me again.

Had I summoned her up again because I saw her yesterday?

Lana…

Lana, here at my house standing there in the lush green grass like it was something she'd always done.

When I parked, glanced at the car once more, then looked back out to her, I realized this wasn't my wild imagination.

It was real.

She was real and as crushed as I was about the past, the sight of her wiped my mind clean of the bitterness.

Seeing her lulled me back to the fascination I'd always had for her.

Fascination and desire nearly drove me insane before we got together.

It was fascination and desire that fueled me as I continued to watch her, and made me want her all over again.

Almost two decades had passed and so much had happened.

So much had happened to me and here I was yet again sucked into the same wild effect she'd had on me.

She was here and she was real.

Back in the flesh here in Wilmington.

The place it all began.

Home.

CHAPTER 6

RYAN

LANA TURNED to face me as I approached.

Uncertainty instantly washed over her beautiful face and in the same instant it took me back to how she used to look and act around me years ago.

Nervous.

To me that was one of the sexiest things about her.

The nerves and uncertainty over what I was going to say and do. I couldn't blame her, people often got like that around me because of my wild ways. No one could tell how I'd react.

Her soft pink lips parted when I stopped in front of her, my gaze clinging to hers. Still trying to process that she was really here.

The beginning of a smile tipped the corners of her pretty mouth but receded back into the uncertainty. She brought her hands together and assumed what I called her public presence. That was what I called it after I found her years ago and noticed that air of confidence about her I'd never seen before. It made her look like a different person.

After I'd found her I spent far too much time trawling the internet, looking her up. Trying to see what she'd done with her life and herself.

All the images I'd found showed her change, and almost slip into a mask, becoming the strong woman she presented to the world. Completely different to the little shy girl I used to know.

"Hi." She spoke first.

"Hello." Although I answered it felt like an automated response I was set to give by default.

"Please, don't throw me off your property. I know I have no right to be here." She gave me a half shrug. "I don't have any right to be here at all, or probably to speak to you. I just wanted you to know I'm back. Back here in Wilmington for the investigation. Turns out the police were trying to find me but that name change of mine made it a little challenging. I... um didn't want you to just see me around town or in passing and well... see me without me doing this part, first." She nodded.

I got what she was saying and appreciated it. I had expected her return. Like her, I would have been on the next flight if I'd gotten the news I served her with yesterday.

"So you came here?" I asked, inclining my head to the side. "You don't owe me anything. If I saw you around I would have assumed the reason for your return was the investigation."

Her shoulders tensed. "I know..." she pulled in a deep breath. "I guess the other reason for my visit was because of that thing I do owe you."

"What's that?"

"An apology."

I groaned inwardly, not knowing what to say.

An apology was an apology. It was an expression of sorrow. While it was a thing that a person could appreciate, it didn't fix anything.

It didn't mend damage done, and it didn't resolve anything other than to give some peace of mind that the person who hurt you was sorry they did it.

The bitterness inside me wanted to ask her if she thought an apology was sufficient but I held off. It was like Dad said, she must have had her reasons for leaving. Reasons I wasn't privy to.

I was just cut deep because it felt like I was the one she left. We were leaving anyway, but she left me behind.

"Ryan." She held my gaze with a strong intensity. "I am truly sorry for all that happened. I know it's not enough. An apology isn't enough, but it's something I needed to do."

I stared back at her, unable to tell her that I accepted the apology, because I didn't.

I didn't accept because there was still so much she wasn't saying. It was in my nature to hold on to a grudge until it killed me. What countered that was that damn desire and fascination I'd always had for her.

It told me she was here, expressing her sorrow to me for hurting me. The girl of my dreams was here in front of me as real as the sun setting behind us, and if I could still think of her as the girl of my dreams then maybe I could give her a chance.

"Do you want to come in?" That was my attempt at breaching my stubbornness. "For a drink... I still make Amelia's sweet tea. Habit."

The light in her eyes sparkled and she nodded, giving me that beautiful smile I first fell for when I met her at eight years old.

"I'd love that. I'd really love that."

I turned to walk to the house and she fell in step with me.

When we got inside I noticed the way she scanned the place. I hadn't been here long. It was a month shy of a year. I'd moved out of the house I'd bought when I'd married Tiffany the second I found out Jack wasn't mine.

Pain and hurt drove me away because I couldn't believe how low Tiffany had stooped. We'd had such an argument I don't know how I didn't kill her.

I'd found out the truth by accident when we were going through some documents in the attic. I came across her hospital records from when she had Jack. She liked keeping stuff around, even stuff I didn't see any point in keeping. It was why I was in the attic.

I was going through the wad of paperwork and I didn't know what the hell made me take note but I saw that Jack was blood type O. I was type AB. I'd never thought about it before but the red flag waved itself in front of me big time.

Then a paternity test confirmed it. A test confirmed I wasn't the father to a child I loved with everything in me.

I led Lana into the living room. I had an open plan kitchen that led out here.

She walked over to a painting on the furthest wall and stopped to admire it. She knew it well. It was the last painting I'd done when we were together. What she

75

didn't know was it was the last painting I'd done in the last seventeen years.

She turned back to face me with a little smile on her face. She was eighteen then. I did that painting a few days after her birthday. We'd just come back from the first real getaway. Everyone thought we were somewhere else. Her on a school trip. Me back at college. Really we spent the weekend together at a hotel in Charlotte.

We never left the bed.

Thinking back now, I know with absolute certainty her mother would have skinned me alive if she'd found out what I'd gotten up to with her barely legal daughter, but I would have done it all over again.

I'd made love to her, and it was then I got the idea for us to go away. It wasn't the first time we were together, it was just the time that mattered the most and the first of the many times I'd had her that I classed it as making love.

"I remember this," she stated with reminiscence.

"Yeah?"

"Hmmm hmmm. I still say it looks a lot like the woodland near Charlotte."

"It's the woodland near the mansion," I maintained. It was a silly argument we'd had running.

She pointed to the painting and focused on the little

gate at the start of the woods. It had a red ribbon looping through the chain.

"We saw something similar in Charlotte," she noted.

"Coincidence." I blinked.

When I did the painting I was thinking of a man I used to see walking his dog through that woodland area. The dog liked anything red. One day the dog went missing and the man started leaving red ribbons around the place in an attempt to guide it home.

He never found it. My theory was it got stolen. It was a Siberian Husky that was probably worth a pretty penny. I thought it was cool how he left the ribbons so I included one in the painting. By pure coincidence we saw a gated area in the woods in Charlotte that looked exactly like that.

When she looked around the room and saw stuff still packed in boxes, curiosity filled her face.

"I'm busy. Haven't had much time to sort those out," I tried to explain and leaned against the wall.

She faced me. "I know what that's like. Some weeks see me in at least three different countries. It's nice but sometimes I never feel quite relaxed, like you would at home."

I recalled how she'd dreamed of travelling. I was genuinely happy she got to travel. I would have asked more in relation to that if not for the looming questions in my mind.

"When did you get here?" I asked.

"This morning. My friend came with me. Her name's Georgie, she's kind of like the sister I never had."

Sounded like the friend she never really had too. Lana used to keep herself pretty much to herself and those she had as friends were more like acquaintances.

Just girls she spoke to from school or whose parents worked for mine. She never really got close to anyone though.

"That's nice. And... me. How'd you find me?" I would have thought she'd go back to the mansion.

"Same way you found me... I have my ways."

I couldn't help the smile that pulled at the corner of my mouth. "Lana D'Angelo has a big office in LA. Her own fashion house. I just looked up the address on Google. Pretty certain that wasn't how you found me."

Again she brought her hands together. "No... I got a private investigator."

"Didn't know I was worth all that trouble, and man you worked fast. You know my parents still live at the same place, you could have just gone there." I smirked without humor.

"No," she breathed. "I just... wanted to see you. I just wanted to know where you lived. It felt better this way to just see you."

"How long will you be in town?"

She shrugged. "I don't know. I figured I'd come see what was happening and then decide. I'd like to stay for the whole investigation. However long it might be. I have my work covered back in LA, plus I'm sure many would agree I'm due a vacation."

Since no one knew how long this investigation could take or anything really about it, her length of stay could be anywhere from a week to a month. Or more, or less.

I looked at her and couldn't believe this was what happened to us.

Her standing over there by my painting and me here not touching her. After the first time I kissed her, I couldn't keep my hands off her, couldn't think straight, couldn't think about anything else besides kissing her again and tasting her sweetness. Raw honey and wild strawberries, that was what she tasted like.

"I'm going to make that tea." I gave her a curt nod and she could tell I wasn't okay. It was in her eyes. At least it seemed like she still knew me in that way.

I went to the kitchen, made the tea and tried for less tension when I went back out.

We sat in the sitting room near the fireplace I was hoping to start using. I didn't use it last year because I couldn't get into the feel of the place. I didn't really think I could justify a fire either, with the weather moderately warm.

This area of the house always reminded me of my parents' place. They had a room just like this, but more conservatory style. Amelia called it the summer room. Every evening she used to get the two of us and make her sweet tea and some kind of pastry.

I could cook but I wasn't the kind of guy to bring out the baking tins so that part was lost on me. The tea though reminded me of her. She used the time to check on us and made sure we were okay.

Mom was always doing something for the million and one charities our family sponsored and Dad was always busy. Most evenings never saw them at home. Weekends were filled with socials and parties. It gave me room to get up to all manner of shit.

"So," Lana began, her voice breaking the silence. "You became an attorney."

I nodded. "Yeah, seemed like the thing to do. Fall in line."

"You did good. I always knew you would, and I'm sure with your creativity you still paint the most amazing pictures."

"I don't paint anymore," I informed her.

She looked taken aback by that and probably displayed more emotion in relation to that than anyone else ever had.

Dad asked me about it but like with everything he was very careful with what he said. Mom was happy about it, happy when she realized I'd stopped. She never said as much, I could just tell.

"Why?" she asked.

"Too busy." No point telling her that I lost my inspiration with her departure.

"To paint?" She looked at me in disbelief.

"A lot changed when you left Lana. I changed too. There was stuff I had to focus on, things like painting took up too much time."

"Oh... I'm sorry."

"Yeah, me too. There are a lot of sorrys in this house tonight."

The tension came back and weighed heavily on me. It was hard to just sit here and not ask even one of the million questions that swirled through my mind.

Her hands tensed around the cup handle and she set it down.

"Maybe I should go... I don't want to upset you, and being invited into your home is more than I'd hoped for." She stood up and I stood too, but not before slamming down my cup.

"What did you expect by coming here?" I narrowed my gaze at her.

"I don't know... I don't... know. I was just hoping we could talk."

"*Talk?* About what? I have so much to say to you,

and I feel like I can't say it without ripping into you for leaving."

"Ryan all I can do is apologize."

"Apologies like the one you're trying to give me are usually accompanied with an explanation. Even some shit like: *I'm sorry I left I had this to do, I'm sorry I left I had other plans, I'm sorry I left I never really loved you.*"

"No." She gasped. "That wasn't it, that wasn't why."

"Then tell me, tell me the reason. Lana, you just disappeared and no one knew where you went. You just disappeared on me months after your mother died. For all I knew the grief could have gotten to you so bad that you did the same thing she did." I didn't mean to say that but it just came out. Of course that had crossed my mind. For a time I believed it. I felt the only thing that could have kept her away from me was death.

"I can't explain, and I knew what it must have looked like to you. I had my reasons for leaving but it was never because I didn't love you, or want the plans we had. Being with you would have been what I wanted most."

"You say that to me now, but I find it hard to believe."

She blew out a steady breath. "Ryan, sometimes things happen and you have no control. You do what's best, you do what you can, you do what you have to whether you want to or not."

There was something in the way she said that, that got to me.

"Maybe me leaving was for the best, for you… look at you," she added. "You did good. You did really good working with your father. I'll bet you really made your parents proud of you. I just hope… hope. I hope we can still be friends."

Friends?

I just stared at her. She hung her head down and saddened filled her eyes when I didn't answer.

I felt like an idiot as she pressed her lips together and I watched her leave. Leaving me like she was never really there. Just like the figment of my imagination that would fade away.

Her leaving was never for the best, not for me. Not once did I think that. All that talk and still no explanation.

No reason why.

I would have accepted if she said she left because she was grieving over Amelia and wanted to start afresh, but she never said that.

Fuck. I would have even accepted if she said she didn't love me, but she said it wasn't that.

So what was it then?

Why couldn't she just give me a straight up answer?

And friends…

Really?

The problem about that was, we were never friends. That wasn't us.

Never started that way and never ended that way either.

I'd never been a friend. That was always clear.

CHAPTER 7

LANA

EIGHTEEN YEARS AGO...

"Tell the truth, looks bad doesn't it?" Mr. O'Shea asked tilting his head to the side.

He looked at the two shelves he'd just put up for me. I was certain they were supposed to be straight and not lopsided. Also, that the hinges were supposed to go under the shelf, not on top, and quite possibly they weren't supposed to rock from side to side.

I however was far too happy to care what my new shelves looked like.

I was just happy to have them.

"They're perfect," I bubbled, clasping my hands together.

He looked to me and tapped my head the way he used to when I was little. I was a few months away from my seventeenth birthday and he still did the same.

"Such a sweet girl, pretty sure your mother told you not to lie though." He smirked. When he did that he looked exactly like Ryan.

A tamer version of him with the good natured vibes of someone like Cary Grant, or Frank Sinatra when he was in Singing in the Rain.

God, listen to me, I blamed Mama for her classic Hollywood obsession.

Conrad O'Shea was actually more like my fairy godfather. A fairy godfather minus the wings and the magical dust.

And no, I wasn't lying. I did think the shelves were perfect.

"They are perfect. Just what I need." I gave him a bright smile.

He looked like he didn't believe me.

"Sweet girl, just let me know if they fall down. I think I should have gone with a carpenter." He frowned as he looked over at the shelves and brought his hand up to dark mane of hair. "In fact I think I'd prefer to get someone in to remodel the room for you."

"That is far too much. I like it just the way it is." I nodded with excitement while he looked around the attic with his lips upturned.

He'd given me the attic as a working space. It was a sort of present for winning the new talent competition in Belle Magazine and having my dress featured in their last issue.

I was still running around in heaven with delight. It was the first thing I'd ever really achieved. Mama bought me a sewing machine and I had massive plans. Seriously massive plans.

"Lana, I have to admit you have some strange taste. Room looks awful. Just terrible. When I said you could have it I meant I'd fix it up for you. As it is, it's little better than something from that creepy movie Ryan loves."

I laughed. "Friday The 13th?" I couldn't believe that's what he meant but it was.

He nodded. "Yup, the one and only."

I was so excited when he said I could have the room up here that I did my own tidying. Sure it might not be all that, and there was still a lot to be done but it worked for me. He put the shelves in thinking it would help, and it did.

I loved that he was so kind to me and always had

that fatherly presence. It was what I imagined my own father to be like.

"You guys still up here?" Mama asked, walking in. She carried a feather duster and the smile on her face was infectious. She was so proud of me.

"Yes, Amelia please tell our girl she needs a better office than this," Mr. O'Shea said, when Mama slipped her arm around me.

She laughed. "You know how grateful we are. It's more than we could hope for. A whole room just to sew in."

"You know I'll do anything... for both of you." He nodded and there was a twinkle that sparkled in his eyes as he looked from me to her.

"Yes... *apparently*." Came Kathy O'Shea's voice.

She stood at the door and while she smiled, the disapproval was in her eyes.

When she looked at Mama and me she gave us what I called a fake ass smile. Phony as hell and cold. *Fake.*

I may have chided myself for comparing people to Classic Hollywood actors, but I didn't think I would be wrong in associating Kathy O'Shea with Blanche Dubois from A Street Car Named Desire. People were always telling her how much she'd looked like Vivien Leigh, who'd played the character.

It was actually true. Kathy didn't just have the same striking appearance she came with the Blanche Dubois accent too because she was from the high society of New Orleans. Her arctic personality, however did not match her beauty.

Her old stuff was up in here, nothing grand in particular. Just a few boxes here and here that were moved down to the basement. She never even came up here and as far as I knew didn't have any plans for the room, it was just evident from her attitude that she didn't really want me having it.

"Apparently, even when I listed the plans I had for the room," she added.

Mr. O'Shea gave her a tight-lipped smile. "Yes, even so. I just thought the room could be put to better use than for storing old newspapers and magazines."

Mama tensed next to me. She'd always tensed up, almost standing to attention when Mrs. O'Shea was around. I hated that she felt she needed to do that.

"Okay, dear." Mrs. O'Shea said cutting off any further comments from him. When she looked back to me that smile returned. "Well anything to support talent. It's nice to see magazines like Belle giving the young people of today a chance to shine."

"Thank you Mrs. O'Shea. Maybe I could make you a nice shawl to wear to the festival." That was me always and ever the girl who tried, even with people who didn't like me.

She tilted her head to the side and regarded me with

a softer, kinder smile. "That would be lovely dear. I'd like that." She returned her focus to her husband and the tautness in her expression came back. "Conrad, we have dinner with the Pederson's at seven, best not to hang out here too long. I don't want to be late."

With that she walked away, leaving behind a tension even though my attempt probably lessened the pull of the atmosphere.

Mama looked to Mr. O'Shea, worry on her face.

"Conrad, if this upsets your wife, you really mustn't give us this room," Mama said and I died a little inside.

He shook his head. "No, don't mind her. You know what she's like. Don't even worry about it." He smiled down at me. "Lana, enjoy your room. Don't unpack too much, I've decided I'm going to get that carpenter after all." He looked around the room and smiled wider. "We can have a work station over there for your thinking space, some rails over there and a couple of mannequins."

I gasped in surprise and deep gratitude. Instinct made me rush to his arms. It was the thought of the mannequins. That was the cherry on top. I hugged him, it was the first time I'd ever hugged him. He hugged me back and tapped my head.

"Vogue." He smirked pulling away. "Dior, Chanel, Armani, Versace. Show them how it's done kid. The Lana Connell way."

Inspiration swept over me and I experienced that pride in myself that I longed for.

"Thank you. Thank you so much," I gushed.

He straightened up and looked at Mama. "Don't work too hard Amelia."

She nodded.

One last smile at the both of us and he left too.

"I'm proud of you Lana," Mama said. "I really am. You're going to be somebody big one day. This is just the beginning."

"Thank you for everything. Without you I wouldn't even have this dream." I was going to wait to tell her my plans but right now felt like the perfect time. When we talked about college she'd just assumed I'd go somewhere I could study fashion design. She never knew I was aiming for a specific school like Parsons and I wouldn't dare tell her because of the expense. I'd only ever talked about it in passing because it was the best. I never told her I dreamed of going there. Things had changed with this new found recognition I'd received. It might really be a possibility now.

"You are very welcome my girl. I'm grateful for you too."

"Thank you. Mama, I'm going to try and apply for the summer school at Parsons," I chirped with excitement.

"*What!*" Her hands flew up to her cheeks.

BELLA FONTAINE & KHARDINE GRAY

"I just have to do a collection, something inspiring and creative. Applications close in March. You need to have won some award to apply and now that I have, I have a shot."

She squealed with delight and we both started jumping up and down and screaming. Screaming like I'd actually gotten accepted. The thing was if I got into the summer school, I'd have a shot at getting in to study there the following year. Or, maybe even a scholarship.

"Oh my God girl you are full of surprises." She hugged me hard and held me there. "Well done Lana. You got this."

I think I did.

I really thought I might have a shot so I was going to try.

My attempts to try began the following day at five a.m.

I got up and cleaned the library and the hall. I had a rigorous schedule set out that left no room for error.

That meant focus, focus, focus. And, it also meant ignoring the shadow that had been lurking around me for the last couple of weeks.

The shadow a.k.a Ryan O'Shea.

I hadn't spoken to him properly in several months. Not since that day I went to thank him for the fabric. That was September last year. It was January now.

He didn't even join Mama and me for our usual

suppertime sweet tea. It was like he'd decided he was too old for that and had better things to do. He'd stopped just before he did his SAT's. Mama made up the excuse that he must have been studying, but we both knew Ryan never studied a day in his life. Unlike people like me the guy didn't need to. He aced everything and aced his SAT's without blinking.

When I did see him it was in passing, a glimpse in the corridor at school, out on the field playing football, or sitting in the quad with Tiffany either glued to his lap or his mouth like she was a permanent extension of him.

That part.... *God* ...ugh, I always felt like giving myself a kick up the backside because during all the other times I'd glimpsed him I'd always felt his eyes on me, watching me. He just never talked to me. I didn't know how to explain it.

My work was a much needed distraction and so wonderful to get lost in.

I made my sketches all that week when Mr. O'Shea got the carpenter in to revamp the room. It looked like something from one of the high end dramas I'd seen Mama watching, where the women were lady bosses and had their own offices.

It made me feel so important and special, like I'd already made it as a designer.

With the sketches done I just had to create my

design. The criteria was a collection of three pieces of clothing of varying style inspired by something you found intriguing. For me that was the combo of seasons and emotions. I chose autumn for the glorious color that surrounded us and the emotion was love.

I worked day and night on them perfecting everything until I had three of the most gorgeous dresses I'd ever seen in my life.

Three gorgeous dresses I'd designed and sewed. Three gorgeous dresses that looked like they were ready for the red carpet.

You just had to look at them and you'd be able to see that I'd worked with my heart and soul.

It took me over two months to complete them.

The last Saturday of March came and I was just doing minor finishing touches.

It was bordering on eleven and I planned to treat myself to an episode of Smallville and a giant bowl of deluxe chocolate ice cream with chocolate sprinkles when I was done.

Earlier today I'd gone over the hem work and perfected everything. I was just doing my final scan of perfection. The project was due Friday. I wanted to spend the rest of this week giving my portfolio one last proof so I'd planned for today to be the deadline on the dresses.

In my over the top way I'd spent the whole evening

going over each dress from bottom to top. I was doing the same again for one last check when I stopped at the first dress in the collection and mulled over the inspiration I'd thought about when I first did the designs.

It was a perfect sleeveless dress with a plunging neckline and built in bra. The length flowed down to the ground and looked like something out of a classic Hollywood film. Like something Audrey Hepburn would wear. It had just the right amount of class and sexy mixed in one.

The color was what I called wildfire and the silk fabric gave it that mysterious sass.

When I'd started designing it I'd wondered if I should give it a slit up the side. It was one of those things that crossed my mind because it looked like it suited it, but I just wasn't sure. I thought, if anything, the last dress that was a dark blood red should have the split because it was love in full bloom.

"Is this where you live now?" Ryan's voice pierced the silence in the room and made me jump.

I whirled around to face him and saw that he'd been standing by the door, resting against the frame. In his black leather biker jacket and white t-shirt that displayed the wealth of muscles that lined his abs he oozed that bad boy attitude like he owned it.

I wasn't sure how this was possible but he seemed

more handsome than ever. So like always the shyness returned to me and I didn't know what to say to him.

"I'm working," I answered.

I set down the case of pins I'd been holding on the worktable and returned my attention to him. Him with his penetrative stare.

"Can see that princess, just wondering if you've decided to live up here now."

My deciphering of his words was that I hadn't really been around at all over the last two weeks. I'd done what I needed to in the house and at school and headed straight up here when I was finished. The regimented schedule I had prevented me from seeing much of anyone. So... I actually hadn't seen him either.

"I'm surprised you noticed. You don't actually speak to me unless you need something." I didn't know where my voice came from but it was there when I needed it, probably as a result of my mind being free from the confusion and mystery of him for the last few weeks.

When he chuckled deep and low, it stirred something in the pit of my stomach.

My nerves spiked when he stepped away from the door frame and came inside the room.

It being the first time he'd been in here made me nervous as hell.

Everyone had seen my dresses, even Mrs. O'Shea. And even with her cold mannerisms, she complimented me on the work I'd done. She was a tough cookie to crack and her words encouraged me. If however, Ryan told me my dresses looked like shit I knew it would hurt me deeply.

He walked around the mannequins and surveyed each dress in silence. The silence amplified the anxiety a hundredfold and I swear I died the same amount of times as I continued to watch him.

Then I died one last time when he said nothing.

What the hell was he thinking? I didn't know anyone who looked at something for so long and just said nothing.

"What is it called?" he asked.

"What?" My heart squeezed.

"It's art, you must have a name for it."

I sighed and narrowed my eyes at him. "The Prelude to a Kiss."

It was like the 90's movie. That was where I got the name, to me it looked and felt just like that.

"*Prelude?*" he asked in that taunting manner that annoyed the hell out of me.

"Prelude. You know like the buildup. The thing that comes *before* and you know the end result is going to be amazing, because you had a taste." Said me the girl who'd never been kissed.

He stepped closer and slanted his head, allowing his longish locks to drift to the side.

97

"Is that how you kiss?" He looked at my lips which I was sure needed Chapstick. I was sure that my lips were currently as dry as my throat had become in response to his question.

Now... what was the right answer? If I said yes, he'd say something weird. If I said no, he'd say something weird. If I said something else, he'd say something weird.

"That is how I imagine a kiss should be." I declared but the sinful smile on his face told me I'd fallen straight into his trap.

He took another step to me, straightening up this time. "So, you're saying you don't know, but that's what you imagine it to be?"

I just stared at him.

Why couldn't he just leave well enough alone when he asked me the name of the collection? Why the grilling?

"It's imagination, that is what designing is. It's not that deep." I moved away from him, deciding to ignore him and hoped he might go away.

He didn't though. He came right around to me and stood closer than I liked.

"There is no prelude to a kiss. It just happens," he declared.

"Ryan... what is wrong with you?" I placed my hands on my hips and frowned at him.

"Nothing." A slow easy smile spread across his sensual lips.

"Okay, then just leave my work alone. Like you said it's art so I can call it whatever I want. If I think it's a damn prelude to a kiss that is what it is. I get that you've done enough kissing to write a book on it but I didn't ask for your opinion. My work is what I imagine kissing to be like, and that's it."

His smile widened. "There's that word again."

"What word?"

"*Imagine.*"

I gazed at him and felt the combo of fury and weakness I'd always felt around him. This conversation was perhaps the longest we'd ever had, but, previously he didn't need to talk to me for any length of time to know how to get to me.

This guy knew me.

The more he looked at me the darker his eyes became and I got that sensation I'd felt months ago in the garage.

One step toward me, and I stepped back. Another step and when I stepped back I was against the wall.

Just like last time, he placed his hands either side of me, and just like before he leaned in close like he was going to kiss me. This time though he moved to my ear and lingered there.

"You've never been kissed, have you... *Lana?*" His

voice was like a gentle caress of a languid summer breeze that beckoned you to its will.

He shifted and hovered inches away from my face, making my heartbeat speed up until it was racing.

"That's not important," I breathed.

"It is."

"Why?"

"Because…" he inched closer. "When I kiss you, you'll see there is no prelude. The kiss simply is."

All I heard was the first part of what he said. I experienced what I imagined people spoke of when they had an out of body experience. Like they were looking on themselves and what was happening. In my case it felt like that but it felt more like some kind of dream. Not real.

It became real though, when he leaned closer and in one smooth motion covered my lips with his. As his lips pressed to mine a blast of energy washed over me, over me and through me, consuming and raging like fire with an infernal heat.

I closed my eyes savoring the taste. The taste of him, it was nothing compared to what I thought kissing would taste like, and not what I imagined kissing him would taste like.

It was so much more.

And… he was right. The was no prelude.

The kiss simply is.

This kiss was exactly that, and it continued. When he swept his hot wet tongue into my mouth my knees gave out and the air left my lungs, leaving me weightless.

Breathless.

In response, Ryan slipped his hand behind my head, lacing his fingers through my hair, pulling me flush against the firm wall of his chest which was exactly as hard as it looked.

A soft moan left my lips and he kissed me harder, then pulled away without warning, leaving me gasping for air. *For him.*

My eyes widened with shock as I gazed at him, while he just gave me that cool smile. If not for the desire in his eyes and the slight hint of color to his cheek I would have thought that kiss had no effect on him.

"There... Now you know. Change the name and come and tell me. I may show you my artwork then."

I watched him pull a cigarette from his back pocket and tuck it behind his ear, then he walked out, leaving my lips burning with fire.

I narrowed my eyes and pulled in a deep breath to clear my head.

Ryan O'Shea just kissed me...

Ryan O'Shea just gave me my first kiss *and...*

It was no mere kiss.

It was the kind a girl needed to book a week in confessional for, because of the sinful, sexual things that tarnished my mind.

Ryan O'Shea just kissed me,

And…

What was that he'd said about his artwork?

CHAPTER 8

LANA

PRESENT DAY ...

I walked over to the cupboard in the kitchen and placed a set of china plates inside with the other dinner wear.

The oil painting of the landscape on the wall next to the cupboard reminded me of Ryan's painting. The house and surroundings reminded me too of the landscapes he liked to do.

I'd probably picked it based on that. I was just glad it

was available immediately and the owners didn't mind a rental with a flexi-stay.

I always opted for houses rather than staying in hotels because I was away over such long periods of time.

This house was a two story Georgian- style home with a front porch that overlooked the river. As it wasn't far from The Cape Fear Coast, in the distance was a scenic view of Wrightsville Beach.

It was what I called comfortable and the period furniture inside enhanced the vibe.

Georgie and I got here early yesterday morning, unpacked and the private investigator I hired got back to me with Ryan's details.

I may have been a mess after seeing Ryan back in L.A. but I'd decided that the first thing to do when I got here had to be to see him. I wanted to do that no matter what the outcome would be, or how his reception of me turned out. It felt right and so did the apology. That was all the things I'd planned out in the short space of time, while Georgie did everything else with the house.

The minute the P.I. came back to me I looked over the details. My stupid heart tapped into my teenaged self when I saw he was listed as divorced.

While it saddened me that he'd gone through a divorce, in the back of my mind I'd thought of how someone else had my guy.

It was so irrelevant in the grand scheme of things. Seventeen years. A lot had happened. At least he got married, even if it didn't work out. Me on the other hand had serial dated. That was child's play, worse when he was my benchmark that no one had managed to reach.

Nobody at all.

Ryan was *the* guy, and a century could have passed and he'd still be the only guy to reach me the way he had.

I'd thought about him non-stop since I'd left his house yesterday.

Memories of us and what used to be filled my head. For some reason I had

the memory of our first kiss stuck there.

That first kiss.

My first kiss, and the first of many with Ryan.

Maybe it was the first time that I'd felt my heart awaken and it changed my creative spark.

I had an hour before I had to go to the station to meet with Detective Gracen.

I was ready to go and ready to see what had instigated the need to reinvestigate my mother's death.

At the same time, here I was thinking about where Ryan and I began, as if I could do something about it.

When people said you could be more effective in your pursuits if you'd experienced something they weren't joking. He kissed me and somehow I knew more than I had prior to the kiss.

It made me change the name of my collection within seconds after. From 'The Prelude to a Kiss' to 'The Kiss'.

And as I explained in the portfolio summary what the collection was about the words had poured from me.

I submitted my work the Friday of that week and I'd expected to hear back from the course administrator at Parsons within six weeks. When I heard from her three days later offering me a placement in the summer school I didn't know what to do with myself. The offer was accompanied by a personal message expressing how impressed she was with my work, and the artistic value of how I described a kiss.

It was the first time in my life that I'd experienced true happiness.

Happiness that stemmed from a kiss a boy gave me that set off a chain reaction of everything.

I went to summer school at Parsons that year and it was the best experience of my life. I'd ended up getting the scholarship too for the following year. I landed it hands down with another collection I designed. By then I was so wrapped up in Ryan the inspiration flowed from me like a river. It came easier than before the kiss. My talent was natural of course but when he was in my life the inspiration poured from my soul.

I knew my visit yesterday had probably achieved nothing.

No answers or anything solid I could give him. I knew that and I was hoping I could say something that would carry enough weight to be a sufficient answer.

But... there was no answer that was more acceptable than the truth.

And, I couldn't lie and say that I didn't feel more hurt than I already was when he never gave me a response when I asked if we could be friends.

Again, that was something I should have expected. It was a foolish thing to say given the circumstances. Very foolish and me pushing the limit on something I shouldn't.

I most likely would have been the same as him, and honestly he'd shown more compassion than I would have if the tables were turned. What he wanted was the truth.

He never knew what happened to me.

Never knew how I fell off the path of life.

I never went to Parsons. When I left home I was so lost and broken.

I headed to L.A., and got a job waitressing. It wasn't until six months after that I found some resemblance of myself as I skimmed through a fashion mag.

It made me sign up to The University of South California to start the following year. That was where I'd met Georgie and later got a bigger opportunity in my senior year to do a year's placement in Milan at Dior.

That was how my story went. How it all happened and things just sort of took off. All good, but it was like that night when I got my first kiss.

Everything I'd done at the time on my collection was good then he kissed me and it became better. That line was the difference between being good and being the best. Being good and being great.

Georgie came into the kitchen, pulling me from my thoughts.

She gave me a warm smile when she saw me by the window and lowered to sit on one of the high stools behind the counter.

"Hey, you okay?" she asked resting perfectly manicured fingers on the countertop. Her nails were the same pewter color as the granite surface.

"Yeah, just sorting out the rest of stuff." I waved my hand over to the little box of cleaning supplies the custodian had left us.

"I can do that later. You sure you don't want me to go to the station with you."

That concern filled her eyes again. She'd asked the same question earlier when I got the appointment with Detective Gracen.

"I'm sure. I'll just go check things out and come back." Maybe it was stupid to go by myself. I just wanted to see what I was up against first before I involved her. I couldn't explain it other than the fact that it had stirred up all the emotions I'd felt from back when Mama died. The same thing was happening now.

"Lana, I'm here to support you. This feels like something I should be going to. Please don't stop me from helping you."

I sighed and moved to join her around the counter.

"We've never spoken about your mom too much. I know it's hard for you and I've tried my best to respect that. But... what if it is something serious? This is why I'm here and I'll be here as much as I can during this time. I don't want to alarm you but the thought of you getting some news that's difficult to hear worries me."

I sighed and nodded. "Okay... I see what you mean. And yes, I think maybe I could do with the support."

She was going to be here until Sunday so I had her for the next few days. Truth be told I needed her support for so many things.

"Good."

"I just wish I knew what it could be. I'm eager to find out what's going on but I'm scared of the unknown."

"I know. It's all so odd. My thoughts are that it's gonna be something to do with her death itself."

"She killed herself, Georgie. I don't need to get a refresher on the details."

It was hard enough to accept it. Every time I did I felt that essence of failure again, all over again. I wasn't there for her when she needed me. I was with Ryan. I was with him and every time I thought of what she must have gone through, grief in abundance would take me.

God knew how many support groups I'd attended during college to help me deal with her death, and every time that word –suicide –was mentioned, it just ate away at everything inside me.

"I know. I ... wish I knew what to say. This is so difficult. It's the one thing I've always felt inadequate to help you with," she surmised.

"No, please don't say that. You helped me plenty." She was the only person I've ever opened up to about my past. She still was. No one else knew. So many people drifted in and out of my life. She'd been my constant.

"I wish I could help more."

"You're here. You're here and I appreciate you." I gave her a little smile.

" I know you do. Can I make you something to eat before we go?"

"No, I'm not hungry. I ate plenty last night." I did.

It was comfort eating after I got back from Ryan. I'd had a whole Angel cake to myself and pigged out on a family sized pack of Cheetos. Then I ordered pizza. Thank God I was the kind of woman who couldn't pile on the pounds. What I ate last night was enough food for a week.

"I noticed." She giggled. "So, that being said, I'm gonna go get ready *after* you tell me how last night went with Ryan." Mischief lurked in her eyes.

"Oh God, Georgie. It's best if I don't talk about him." I winced bringing my hand to my temple. I blew out a ragged breath and ran a hand over my hair which I'd placed up in a high messy bun.

"You didn't want to talk about him last night either." She smirked. "*But* you know me. I'm not one to keep my nose out of anybody's business girl."

I smiled, wishing this was one of our lazy day girl chats where it was usually me who was giving the advice.

Georgie wouldn't believe how shy I used to be. The woman I was now was like a completely different person. The woman I was now serial-dated wealthy business men and athletes. Gorgeous and sexy and never specifically anyone who could get close to my heart the way Ryan had.

"I'm not sure what to say." I shrugged.

"Well we know he's single, and works with his

father. Did you get past any other basics?" She looked hopeful.

"We talked and I apologized for leaving him. But really... it didn't go well and it didn't go badly either, in the sense that he didn't throw me out."

She bit the inside of her lip and her shoulders slumped.

I guess I probably started out like I was building up to something that wasn't so bad.

"Oh Lana. I'm sorry. I was hoping that maybe you could be friends, or something... I don't know what I'd do if it was me. I'm still shocked by his mother's behavior and to be honest I'm leaning more on the side that you should just tell him the truth."

Her guidance didn't surprise me. It was something I'd advise her to do too.

"I don't think I should do that. *In fact,* I know I shouldn't do that. It's like Pandora's box. Why open it and let out the demons. Ryan adores his mother. He's the kind of guy who loves his mom and will do anything for her. The fact that she's sick too doesn't exactly lend me any favors. I can't do it."

"But Lana... you still have feelings for him." She pointed out. That was my friend. In true 'cut past the shit and get to the point' style she got to the heart of a situation.

Instead of answering I looked out the window and

gazed out to the beautiful river in my view. The ripple of water on the surface sparkled in the bright sunlight like someone splashed diamonds all over it.

It was the warmth of her hands over mine that returned my focus to her.

"Lana, come on, you can talk to me. I'm not interested in this silence over something that's uber clear. You still love him. I see it as clear as day. I think what you need to acknowledge is that seventeen years have passed. You are like the queen and no one can have any kind of hold on you ever again. Even if you were Lana O'Connor you'd still be great. You can have anything you want, why not go after the guy you lost."

I sighed. "I don't know Georgie. It's complicated. Big time. What Kathy O'Shea did to me was so awful. It was so mean and vicious. What made me take that plunge to go was feeling like I wasn't good enough for Ryan." I pressed my lips together. "I felt like my life was the one that was damaged with the loss of my mother and I shouldn't damage his too. I didn't want to feel like I robbed him of a better life, without me."

"You can't know what his life would have been like. Same as you can't know what yours would have been like. But you have now...you have the time now to change things if you want to."

I held her gaze. "I shouldn't want to. Georgie, I appreciate the talk but realistically I just want to see what's going on here and get home. Get back to my life how it should be." *Without Ryan.*

With an exasperated sigh, she gave me a little nod. "Okay, well… as per usual girl, if you want to talk I'm here. I'm all ears."

"Thank you. It totally means a lot. "

Detective Gracen was a thin wiry looking man with a good-natured smile.

He reminded me of Dick Van Dyke with his thick rimmed glasses. He looked a little like him too. I guessed he was in his mid-sixties but he could have been younger, it was just that his hair was a mixture of white and silver strands.

Georgie and I arrived at the station about ten minutes ago. We were early but he agreed to see us straightaway.

His office was the standard detective's office with filing cabinets, shelves, a cluttered desk with stacks of paperwork he'd shoved to the side to make room for his meeting with us, and a mug of coffee.

He sat before us in a leatherback office chair and leaned forward on to his desk with that smile.

"I'm very happy to meet you both." He looked from

me to Georgie. "May I call you Miss D'Angelo, or is Lana okay?"

"You can call me Lana." I told him with a smile.

"Ahh, well that's even better. Now it's like I know you. You can call me Robert or Detective Gracen, but I hope you won't know me long enough to feel like you know me."

I brought my hands together and tensed. That didn't sound good.

"Okay. That sounds a little off key." I hoped I didn't sound rude.

"I know. It's just my way. Forty years on the force and you realize there's little point making small talk in certain situations." He steepled his fingers and gazed full on at me. "Lana, my area of specialty is unsolved cases. When a death has too many questions or it's been labelled as suicide, it comes to me. I didn't really want to go through too much on the phone with you the other day. One, because there isn't a lot to go through, and two because this is the kind of case where we could dig up a lot of memories or cause painful emotional experiences."

"I understand." I did, I just wished I could be as strong as I was normally. I never went to the police station the last time, it was Mr. O'Shea. He had to deal with all of it. It was him who called me and told me what happened. That was painful enough getting the second-hand experience.

"Good. Now, your mother's case is exactly like that. From time to time we do a review of these cases, especially with the rise of modern technology. It helps us give answers we couldn't find way back when. In your mother's case we found an additional document from the coroner's office that wasn't filed with the final autopsy reports. We can't explain why, but it's something that needs to be looked into. That is what we are doing now."

"What did it say?" I asked.

He gave me a light chuckle. "My dear girl I'm afraid that is where the scientific world and the police world blur for me. My part in this is to reopen the investigation based on finding additional documentation, and speaking with friends, family and employers about it. That part is just formality so everyone is aware that I may need to speak to them further. Some people will probably be questioned."

"*Questioned*? You'll be questioning people?" That did sound curious.

"When a case is reopened we do everything that we need to, and go over what we did in the original investigation. If we find something that requires clarification and we need to speak to a specific person or people then we go through the formal manner of questioning."

I swallowed hard. "Do you think you'll find something? I mean... I know it's ... I know you can't answer that but I feel like there must be some element of suspicion here that there could be more."

His gaze clung to mine. "Lana, I can't answer that right now. I will say that it's in my nature to be suspicious and a document that wasn't included in the original reports is a little suspicious. But that is me, and all I will say at this time. It could however very easily turn out to be something as simple as a fault on our part or at the coroners office. The document and the records on it have to be investigated through the correct processes to ensure everything is filed and classified in the appropriate manner." He paused and inclined his head to the side. "I won't know much more until the report comes back from the labs and only then will I know what exactly to do next, based on the suggestions."

I glanced at Georgie and she took my hand.

"Thank you, thanks for your explanation. I think I just want answers too. I don't know why she would have killed herself." The words caught in my throat and the backs of my eyes stung. "But I accept it. I accept that's what happened. I just wish I could have done something... more."

"Of course. That is completely understandable. Lana, I know you've been asked this before, but in the days leading to her death did you see anything that may have alarmed you. Maybe her behavior changed, or reactions. Or even anyone new hanging around."

I shook my head. "There was no one. My mother kept herself to herself. She wasn't even dating anybody and didn't have many friends. If she was she didn't tell me. I remember two days before she was crying."

"Did you speak to her?"

"Yes. She told me she was worried about my aunt. She was a drug addict and my mom spent her earnings on her, trying to bail her out. It wasn't unusual for her to spend thousands. I figured maybe she'd just had enough of it. She was supposed to be saving for my college expenses. We were always sort of on the breadline because of my aunt. My mom was the kind of person who would worry something would happen if she didn't help. So she helped and helped." That was Mama. That was how she was.

"Where is your aunt now?"

That was a good question. A damn good one. Again I shook my head. "I have no idea."

Aunt Larissa was nowhere to be found when I needed her. Of course she was the first person I'd thought of turning to when Mrs. O'Shea kicked me out, except I couldn't find her anywhere. The number we had for her just rang out to voicemail.

I knew she knew what had happened to Mama and I

figured she was dodging having to take care of me. The only person who would have called her the way I had was me.

She lived in Jacksonville and I'd hoped I could stay with her for a little while, but it was a no go.

"Okay. That's all I have for you today. If you think of anything you think I'd find useful call me, even if you think it may not mean anything, just let me know."

"Yes, I will absolutely do that."

"Are you going back to L.A. anytime soon?"

"No, I'll be here."

My work in L.A. could wait.

Everything could wait. Somehow, deep inside, something stirred. A feeling in my gut that told me Detective Gracen had more than a mere suspicion that he'd deemed a matter of formality.

Something told me it was more than that.

CHAPTER 9

RYAN

"DAD, YOU SHOULD HAVE SEEN ME," Jack said with so much excitement his little cheeks flushed with it. "It was like being in a real game. Like on tv. I was so fast."

"Wow, that sounds unreal." I chuckled looking him over in his tracksuit. This kid was something else. He'd been training this morning and here he was again getting ready to practice with Todd, his equally football-obsessed friend.

It was Sunday afternoon, most kids would be watching tv or playing around with their toys. Not mine.

Five years old and it seemed like Jack had found the thing he loved most in life.

I'd played football up until the end of high school. I loved the game, but I was pretty certain I wasn't anything like Jack at his age.

I guess though that maybe he took after his father, whoever that was.

I hated having thoughts like that.

He was my boy whether DNA called the shots or not. The same blood didn't have to run through our veins to make him mine.

"Dad, you are coming to the game next week right? You won't be busy?" He gave me that worried look he usually sported when he thought I was going to say no to something. It had gotten more prominent after I'd moved out, and definitely occurred a lot more since the divorce.

"You know I will be there little man," I promised. Didn't matter how busy I was, I never missed his games or anything to do with him and I wouldn't start doing it now.

"Yesss." He squeaked, jumping up and down.

I laughed. "Hey, if you jump like that you may throw up."

"I'm fine. I'm so excited."

A car horn sounded, signaling his ride had arrived. That was Barry, Todd's father. Barry used to play for the L.A. Gladiators and had assumed the unofficial role of little league coach.

"See you Dad." Jack barely looked at me, he just ran through the kitchen and left in the cloud of excitement that took him.

When I heard the front door close, the seriousness of why I'd come here today came back to me. I visited Jack at least once a week, or he came to spend the weekend with me. It was all unofficial at the moment but I wanted to make it official.

Just like I knew she would, she came into the kitchen a few seconds after Jack left.

When I looked at her my mind went back seventeen years, actually further than that.

I think I'd gotten up to every sin in the book with her. The asshole I was back then was with her because she was easy, and the asshole that came back to haunt me after I found Lana sought refuge in her.

It was a stupid drunken mistake that led me here. I fell right into the trap she set for me that night I came back from L.A after finding Lana.

It was the night I decided to let Lana go. Let go in my heart. She'd moved on and I knew I had to do the same.

That night I went to a bar drunk off my face and fell straight into Tiffany's little trap. At that point I hadn't been with her for close to thirteen years. All the times she'd seen me when I was with Lana she'd always given me that seething glare. Then after Lana left she tried to get with me several times.

I always told her no. Not that time, however. The time when it counted the most.

Because boy did she ever ensnare me. I didn't know that Tiffany was already a month pregnant when I slept with her and she planned to get with me because I could give her a better life.

Fuck, was I ever screwed.

She tucked a strand of her platinum blond hair behind her ear and came closer.

"I figured you'd want to spend some alone time with him," she stated and pulled out a chair to sit next to me.

I rested against the back of my chair and looked at her. Time to get down to business.

"I want to arrange visitation rights with Jack. I want to do it properly."

Instantly she looked hurt and she straightened up. "Why? Why do you need to do that? You see him enough don't you?"

"Tiffany, this is something I want done properly. If you meet some guy and remarry I don't want to get left in the wind, on the outside looking in. I was hoping you'd make this smooth by agreeing."

"Agreeing to allow you to just see him? So that's it Ryan?"

I narrowed my eyes at her wondering if she really hadn't taken in the full picture of what went down with us.

"I don't think it's wise to drag Jack through court with our problems." I held out my palms. "The divorce was bad enough and hard on him. It became hard from when I moved out."

"So move back in." She brought her hands up to her chests and laced her fingers together. "Give me a chance, give us a chance."

Oh God. I didn't know why she had to do this to herself.

A glint of hope sparked within her eyes in anticipation of my answer. As if I was really going to say yes.

"Tiffany... do you realize what you did to me?" I lifted my chin higher so I could glare at her.

"Of course and I'm sorry. Ryan we were good together, we always were. I've known you forever and you know me. You know I love you. I never screwed around while we were married."

I balled my fists on the countertop because I actually knew that for a lie. I knew of at least one time where she'd been unfaithful. It was someone at her workplace. Carson, who was probably the only friend I had left from high school told me he saw her making out with her boss. They were at a dinner party at the Double

Tree. He'd told me he saw her go up to the pent house suite with him.

I seriously doubted that was to file paperwork.

I knew she was screwing around and I never mentioned it because of Jack. I foolishly didn't want to destroy our family over what I thought might have been a one-time kind of thing. It was amazing that she could sit in front of me and lie.

"I'm not getting back together, Tiffany. I'm not."

She frowned. "It seemed like we were getting on well last week."

"I'm trying for Jack's sake. I need to move past this part of my life and get back on track. I don't want you calling me or making these impromptu visits to the office with hope that we're getting back together. We've been divorced for eight months and it's time to move on."

She stood abruptly and glared at me. "I don't accept that. I don't. I gave you a divorce so you could have the time to do whatever it was you needed to do. I always thought you'd come back to me. Now you want me to let you go, *forever.*"

Her problem was the same one she'd always had. She wasn't used to being told no. She was the great Tiffany Tate, wealthy, beautiful and a guy's dream. No one would dare tell her no and mean it.

I just had more balls than most.

I stood too. "Jack is my focus right now. I hope you'll consider going through the proper channels of me seeing him."

She folded her arms under her breasts and just stared at me.

It was fine, I didn't expect her to answer, and I'd expected this reaction from her. Now she knew where we stood for the future and what I wanted.

I left her standing there in the kitchen and headed into town to get some water sealant for my shed. I would have gone to see Dad next, back at the mansion, but I was beginning to think he'd had enough of me. He met with Detective Gracen three days ago and while nothing much was discussed, I could tell Dad was worried.

He was the kind of guy who wore his emotions on his sleeve and his worry rubbed off on Mom.

No one was talking about the obvious situation that had presented itself but they were worried. Me staying away today was to give them some breathing space.

I knew that Detective Gracen would have spoken to Lana too.

Probably saying the same things he'd said to Dad about the extra document he'd found and alerting her that he may need to speak to various people again.

Dad thought he may have wanted to speak to me too, but so far I hadn't been contacted.

When I got into town I decided to walk the long way to the hardware store.

Off in the distance, on the paved path between the ice cream parlor and the florist, was the beautiful young woman I used to imagine running into on the street.

Lana stood there looking around with her purse slinked over her arm and her phone out like she was checking something.

It was funny how I'd imagined running into her in the past and a version of that was what happened when I saw her in L.A.

I'd gone on the business trip and it was a chance to have a little break from home. She was walking through the hotel lobby with a group of people. I later found out there was a fashion show at the hotel and that was when I found out her details. Her name. Lana D'Angelo. No wonder I couldn't find her as Lana Connell.

In the vision I'd had so many times, when I ran into her we spoke. What happened six years ago was nothing like that. It was me wanting so desperately to run to her and ask her what happened.

It was me thanking God and the host of heaven that she was alive and not dead somewhere. Then it was me walking away from finding her because I realized she had a different life, that didn't involve me, and didn't need me.

The urge to walk away now came.

I definitely admitted that the urge to turn down the path to my left came and I nearly went for it.

But… something inside me stopped me from doing so and made me continue to stare.

She was right there about twenty feet away from me, right within my reach. There to speak to… as *friends*.

That was what she'd said she hoped we could be.

Friends.

Could I try that?

Would a friend take note of the way her body looked in that little summer dress? Her body, different to her teenage body had transformed into what I thought a goddess would look like.

Breasts full and round were perfectly displayed against the tight fabric that clung to her skin. Breasts I remembered very well. From the way her nipples would harden against my tongue to the way the swells would warm against the palms of my hands.

The sharp curve of her waist was always so perfect to slip my hands around. It still was.

Along with the curve running down her hips.

Those legs still looked like temptation. Smooth, satin smooth and long. My body remembered them wrapped around my waist as I pounded into her.

I may have had some strange ways of thinking in the

past because quite frankly I didn't care much about what a lot of people thought of me. But, even I couldn't agree that a friend would be thinking those things about another.

But would I allow that to stop me?

I stood there watching her and I contemplated the answer to that.

I'd contemplated the answer to many things when it came to Lana over the last few days and I tried to accept that she had her reasons for not saying more than she had.

Those reasons were in the past. This was the present, and low and behold the only thing that was the same about then and now was that desire and fascination that made me do things I shouldn't do.

Like the step I'd just taken toward her instead of going left to the hardware store.

CHAPTER 10

LANA

"You know I'm pretty certain if you lean anymore you'll fall over," Ryan remarked.

I snapped my gaze to him and a little breath escaped my lips at the sight of him.

I guess I must have looked pretty strange as I'd leaned over so I could see around the corner by the florist.

A dimple appeared in his left cheek as his lips arched into the beginning of a smile and hope filled my heart even though the smile never really came out in full bloom.

He was talking to me and the angst that I'd seen the other day didn't seem to be there.

"I'm looking for the art shop. The map said it was here. Lily's Art Supplies," I explained.

When he actually smiled it took me back to nights spent in his arms on the beach. I remembered how I used to commit his face to memory.

"Yeah, that's Lily's alright," he confirmed. "She's a florist now, the art thing didn't quite work out for her. I heard she decided flowers were more her thing, although she ended up selling a batch of poison ivy to a few people."

I laughed and his eyes sparkled.

"No way, she did that?"

"Uh huh, you know what people are like here. They get an idea and roll with it, doesn't seem to matter if they have the knowledge or backing to do it."

"Yeah, I remember. Like Tony's Pet Shop."

He laughed now, bringing out the dimples in full force. The vision of him actually made my mouth water. I had to blink to refocus my mind and set my thoughts on cleaner paths.

"Yeah exactly like that."

Tony had caught all these wild animals and decided he'd sell them. I'd wanted a fish. Ryan was twelve at the time and I was eleven. Tony had just opened his store and Mama took us both in, thinking it would be cool to get my fish there.

When we saw the crocodile in the tank by the entrance, a python in the tank opposite and a vulture in the cage right next to it, we did a U-turn.

The shop was closed down six months after. How he'd managed to stay open for so long was beyond me. Tony was arrested too for keeping wild animals in enclosures without the proper licenses .

"So, is it okay to ask the only guy I know who's into art where I might find an art shop. I need a sketch pad and some pencils. I left everything back in L.A. thinking I wouldn't really conjure anything up while I was here."

He looked me over and looked like he'd decided he was going to help me.

"Why would you leave your tools?" He tilted his head to the side.

"I wasn't thinking straight."

"Clearly… What did you see?" A glint touched his eyes and the bright blue hue seemed brighter. It reminded me of the Caribbean Sea I'd immersed myself in months ago when I did a photoshoot in Jamaica.

My heart skipped a beat when I realized he was talking to me the way he used to. It was the way one creative person talked to another. A sort of language you shared between you.

I beamed up at him. "A bird flew at the window this

morning and it had the most amazing blue and green undertone to its wings. It flew over the lake and dived into the undergrowth. It reminded me of passion." I'd discovered along my journey that my designs were all inspired by some kind of emotion. "I wanted to do some sketches of the designs that came to my mind."

"Passion?" he asked in that true cocky Ryan style.

I nodded. "That's what I'm calling it for the moment."

"Sounds good."

I widened my eyes at him. "What? You're actually agreeing with me? You never agree with me."

"Well looks like you learned. Cut the shit out and flesh out what you mean to say. No more preludes."

No... no more preludes.

"I figured that passion simply *is*." I borrowed his words from so long ago and he looked at me like he knew what I meant. Like he remembered our first kiss too.

"It is... Come." He turned and started walking, glancing over his shoulder once at me.

I smiled and followed him.

"Is this for a new show?" he asked.

"Not sure yet. I've only just really taken off with my new line. I'm hoping that Fashion Week will get me the exposure I want. So I want something to follow that up with. Something amazing and different."

He chuckled. "And what does Lana D'Angelo consider to be amazing and different?"

"I don't know, maybe feathers." I had that damn bird stuck in my head.

He glanced at me with raised brows. "Feathers?"

"I'll know when it comes to me."

"I feel you already know what you want and it's not feathers. Why don't you just do what you want to do?"

I tucked a wayward lock of hair behind my ear. It had been so long since I'd had someone to talk to like this.

"Leather... I see leather," I confessed. "But colorful leather. Like turquoise and gold. Kind of like tapping into a seventies vibe meets the modern. I just don't know how to pull it off yet. But feathers are in this season," I explained.

He stopped, looked at me in the wild way he used to and did his habitual step forward. It had been years since I'd followed that with my response of stepping back and I wouldn't do it now.

He leaned close and tilted his head to the side. "The Lana I know wouldn't care about what's in season. Leather is sexy as hell and bleeds passion. It's the thing that happens when chemistry and attraction come together." His gaze held mine in place, frozen in the moments we stood there together. "You should definitely go with leather. It suits you."

"Really? You've never seen me in leather." I couldn't help it. My body remembered him being this close and melted.

He gave me his trademark sexy half smile and tapped the side of his head. "Don't need to Princess. It's here. I memorized your body by heart. I know what you look like in everything."

While he moved back and started walking again, heat flushed over my body in an overwhelming blush from the combo of the way he'd looked at me and what he said.

I fell into step next to him and he glanced over at me, brief but effective. It drew me in and wiped my brain clean of everything, even what I'd come out shopping for.

Georgie went back to LA this morning with the plan to come back next weekend if I didn't hear from Detective Gracen in the week. I got the inspiration to do some drawings and decided to come out. Looked like it was a good call as I doubted I would have seen Ryan otherwise.

We walked on a path in silence for about five minutes then we turned the corner near an Italian Bistro and came to a quaint, quirky little art shop that looked like it was more fitting to be placed in a village.

Like a lot of things here much had changed. I

remembered there being an ice cream parlor at that spot.

We went inside and an old man with a long white beard greeted us. He showed us where the sketch pads were but when I saw everything else, I not only got side-tracked but got sucked into buying as many things as I could fill the basket with.

There were these little beads and trinkets to make jewelry boxes. Glittery this and that, and when I got to the paint section I noticed he had an abundance of colors. Ryan and I must have spent well over an hour in the shop and when we were finished that basket of mine was so full there was no way I was going to be able to carry it all the way back to the house by myself.

I'd walked because I was only ten minutes away. The plan was simply to grab the sketch pad and some pencils but somewhere along the line that had changed and I bought the entire shop.

"Christ woman, did you drive?" Ryan huffed as we stepped outside. He carried the heavier bags of paint and tucked the sketch pads under his powerful arms.

"No, I thought I'd be quick and just grab the pads and pencils."

"Three pads and the rest of the shop." He smirked.

"They were all so pretty, I couldn't resist," I answered in a playful tone.

He shook his head at me. "Where do you live?"

"Ten minutes' walk," I replied, kind of hoping he'd walk with me. Call me crazy and one to shoot myself in the foot, and possibly my heart, but I didn't want to say goodbye just yet.

"So two minutes by car?" he surmised.

"Maybe less."

"I'll drop you off."

"Thank you. Does some sweet tea sound like a good thank-you?" A little hop lifted my shoulders.

"Sweet tea and brownies. I just spent the whole afternoon with you while my poor shed suffers."

I giggled. "Your poor shed?"

"It's fine. It'll live." He winked at me and I followed when he turned to walk toward the car park.

CHAPTER 11

Lana

I T TOOK five minutes to get back to the lake house and that was just because of the traffic.

We went into the sitting room to set down the bags by the fireplace.

Ryan looked around and his gaze landed on the river. I stood next to him and admired it too.

I wasn't that surprised to see him looking so taken with the scenery. It was similar to the setting around his house. I liked his better though. It had a homely feel to it, even though there were unpacked boxes. I think it was just the presence of him that made it feel homely.

It was starting to take effect here as I watched him.

"Nice place," he complimented.

"I liked it when I saw the pictures online," I bubbled. "I didn't have a lot of time to shop around, but this was a good pick."

"Yeah, looks that way. Your friend here?"

"No, she left this morning. She's in marketing and has some new clients she's seeing this week. So, I'm here by my lonesome."

"I'm sure you'll be fine."

"Yeah. I live in an apartment in L.A."

"I always figured you'd be more at home in a house." He smiled.

"I am... that is definitely true. It's time that prevents me from really establishing where I want my home I suppose. I travel a lot." That was probably putting it mildly.

"Are you happy?" he asked and rocked back on his heels.

"Yeah. It's nice. It's how I imagined it when I dreamed of making it."

He inclined his head to the side and smiled. "But?"

"I didn't say but." I grinned.

"Didn't have to. It was there lingering on the edge of that last word."

I gave him a little shrug. He was right, there was a *but,* however any problems I had came with the job.

"I didn't think I was going to be so busy. I like it because there's nothing like doing what you love. It's just super busy."

"Well, I know it's not ideal but maybe you needed this break."

I agreed. "Yeah. You know what else I need?"

"What?"

"To make you those brownies."

I sauntered into the kitchen and he followed with that lingering stare.

I started on the brownies and he watched.

I'd talked a lot about myself today, but I noticed he hadn't said much about himself.

"So, what's it like being a defense attorney?" I asked trying to find something solid to carry a conversation.

He leaned over the counter and stared at me. "Boring as shit."

I stopped beating the eggs to look at him. "I'm sure it can't be that bad. Law's like second nature to you."

"Princess, wasn't I always good at that stuff?" He gave me a wolfish grin and straightened up.

Princess...

He'd called me that earlier.

He always used to call me that. Hearing it made my heart recall the way it used to feel.

"Yeah." I nodded. "You were. I thought you'd be

happy doing that eventually when you saw how good you were."

"No. My dad loves the help. We expanded and it's cool. My mom of course was thrilled."

Of course she was. I would have known that even if he didn't tell me.

"How is she?" I asked in an attempt to gloss over what I truly felt. It was just like the time when I offered to make her that shawl. Boy was I ever clueless on the depth of that woman's hatred for me.

Being sick however, with a thing like cancer, must have been awful for the family and awful for her. So, I had a heart in relation to that. Enough of a heart for me to ask how she was.

"Not that good, she's had a lot of therapy and surgery and it looks like she's just hanging on some days. Right now she's in that in between phase where you can tell she's trying. It's been a long road." The way he answered showed how worried he was.

"I'm sorry. I hope she gets better."

"Thank you." He nodded and we just looked at each other.

He chuckled at the silence. "It's weird isn't it? Us here trying to talk like friends catching up. I have a million questions, and I'm here trying to be selective on what to ask and holding off on stuff about your life I *want* to ask."

"Like… what?" I knew I was leaving myself open to questions about anything. Despite that, I didn't want to spoil the reconnection we'd made by being too guarded.

His gaze deepened. "Lana D'Angelo, the internet is littered with all these guys on your arm. Can't help but feel a certain type of way. Maybe it's my ego. I'm the perpetual alpha who needs a reason to explain why something didn't work out."

It didn't surprise me that he'd seen those pictures of me, but there was that question again. The question of why I left.

Why we didn't work out.

"When you left how long was it before you started… *well*, dating again?" He added.

I knew this guy and knew the real question he was asking. He wanted to know how long before I slept with someone else. If anyone else had asked me that I wouldn't have answered, simply because, with the exception of him, I'd never been with anyone who mattered enough for me to care about that.

There was a time when I was his and he was mine. So I owed him an answer.

"It was five years," I replied. "Five years until I dated anyone, and then seven years before I slept with anyone."

I didn't miss the flash of anger that flickered in his

eyes. It felt like I'd just confessed to cheating, although at the time we were years away from being together.

"Seven years?" he asked. His head tilted to the side then straightened up.

"Yeah." Much as I'd wanted to know how long he'd waited I decided it was best if I didn't know.

"It was eight for me," he declared, almost like he could read my mind.

Admittedly, I was shocked, but shamed filled me because I'd slept with someone before he did. Then guilt came because he'd waited so long.

"Eight?" I said that more to myself than him.

"*Eight.* I looked for you for years. Feels like I'm still looking."

While he did that habitual smirk without the humor the backs of my eyes stung.

All I could do was stare back at him.

Ryan spent years looking for me…

Years.

How I'd hoped he'd forget me.

"I'm sorry." I must have sounded like a broken record.

"Yeah… me too," he answered and I wasn't sure if that meant he was sorry he wasted his time looking or that it happened.

"You found me." I pointed out. "It doesn't feel like it was the other day." In my brainstorm and thoughts of him that was the conclusion I'd come to. When I'd seen him in L.A, he'd acted like he knew more than he showed. Even though what he'd showed was pretty effective to express how he felt.

"It wasn't the other day. Found you six years ago… purely by accident. I wasn't looking. The one time I wasn't looking and there you were. Thought my mind was screwing with me when I saw you walk past me in the hotel lobby at the Hilton in Santa Monica."

My lips parted. "Oh my God."

"It was a fashion show."

I knew from the mention of six years ago which fashion show it was. It was a Dior show, one of my most successful where I really got to shine. He was there and I couldn't believe I'd walked past him.

"Why didn't you say something?" I held his gaze.

He shook his head. "No, I wouldn't have said anything. You looked happy… It was enough. I didn't want to be a reminder of what you ran from."

My gaze dropped to the counter.

This was so awful and I couldn't have felt more torn than I did from the inner turmoil that roiled within me. The truth struggled to fight through the barriers I'd placed up to keep it hidden.

I couldn't hold back the wayward tear that ran down my cheek. I wiped it away quickly and willed the rest to stay away. I couldn't start crying again. Not in front of him.

I looked back to him and saw he was already watching me.

"I didn't run from you," I told him.

"It's okay. Has to be, right?"

"It's not okay."

"But it has to be, can't change the past." Hurt filled his eyes but he did that thing where he just glossed over it with a grin. "So… back to playing catch up. Did you ever get married? All those guys, one of them must have ticked the box. At first I kind of hoped that was why I couldn't find you. I told myself that maybe I couldn't find you because your last name changed. Then I did find you and I realized a version of that did happen."

"I didn't get married." My voice came out in a rasp from the anxiety that swept over me.

"How come?"

"I never got that far with any of them."

"Not even one?" he quirked his brows. "You dated some pretty powerful men, with deep pockets, hard to believe that not one of them were marriage material."

"They were not." We continued to gaze at each other and since we were talking about marriage I obviously wondered what happened to him.

He tore his gaze away from mine, glanced to the countertop surface returned his focus to me. "I'm divorced, but I guess you probably knew that if you hired a private investigator to check me out."

I nodded slowly. "What happened?"

Selfishness made envy course through me again. The same envy I'd faced as a child when I watched him with one girl after another.

What was his wife like?

Maybe like the girls at school who swooned over him.

The pain and hardness in his eyes removed the envy from me. It suggested he was about to tell me something that truly hurt him.

"It didn't work out. It's a ...*long*, long story that ended badly. The kind of shit that made life so much worse than it already was." The pain reflected in every word he uttered. It reached out to me. Remorse flooded my heart and weighed down my soul.

I left because I thought his life would be better. Hearing it wasn't, physically sickened me. I set the bowl down on the counter and allowed my brain to truly process what he'd said.

What did Mrs. O'Shea think of that?

She'd been so adamant that her son could do so much better than me and he should.

I hoped he would. I'd hoped he would find someone to love him, even half as much as I did.

If it was half, I would have been satisfied that he'd

have a happy life. Even if it was a third of the love, it would have been satisfactory.

Hearing that never happened grieved me in a way I couldn't explain and to a depth that enraged me.

I walked around to him and for an instant his gaze sharpened. He measured me with a cool appraising look, and gave me a smile that didn't reach his eyes.

"Don't take pity on me, princess," he stated. "That ego of mine doesn't want to be pitied. I got out of the situation."

"I'm sorry," I breathed. It wasn't pity. It truly was deep sorrow. "I didn't want that for you."

He gave me a curious look. "What did you want for me?"

"Someone who made you happy. Someone who appreciated you and your weirdness." I thought some lightheartedness would help.

"You think *I'm* weird?" He smirked.

"Is that even a rhetorical question?" I smiled back.

"No, of course it's not. I'm not weird. I'm extraordinary." Only he could say something like that.

"Yes, exactly." I continued to stare, bringing back the seriousness to the conversation. "I hoped you'd end up with someone extraordinary too and you'd live in a house where you'd paint every day. Like the landscapes you used to paint. I just wanted you to be with someone who deserved you."

He stared at me and bit the inside of his lip. "That sounds real nice, and I feel like an ass because I can't say I wished the same for you, because I wanted to be that guy for you."

My chest tightened on hearing that and I felt worse than I thought I would.

"You were," I confessed, my voice was barely above the whisper on which I spoke.

"*Were.* That's the thing, right? I *was*…I used to be. I'm past tense."

The right thing to do was lie to him and agree that he was past tense. Georgie's words came right back to my mind though.

Right there in the moment. She'd said I still loved him.

I did.

Never stopped. Seventeen years passed us by and I'd never stopped. A century could fly by in the same breath and it wouldn't change what my heart wanted.

"No," I whispered breathlessly.

He leaned closer. "If that's true Lana Connell, then how did we get here?"

"It's complicated." It was like I was programmed to say that, to give that answer for everything.

"Yes, fucking right." He nodded firmly, face stern with conviction. He stood up and towered over me with his height. "I think we can agree on that. It's complicated. It absolutely is. We haven't been together in seventeen years. You've been with other people. I've been with other people. I should have moved on. I should be able to sit here and at least try to be your friend. But when I look at you, it's hard for me to not touch you."

The sting of his words pierced something. It pierced through that wall I'd placed up to guard my heart and keep myself going.

Nothing was truer than what he just said. I should have moved on too. I thought that I'd taken those first steps many years ago when I stopped checking in on him. I thought I'd done both of us a favor by trying to move on with my life and forget the past.

I didn't though. I never moved on. I just fooled myself into thinking so. Like patching together a broken vase with tape. It may hold together but it would never be fixed.

Touch...

I released the breath I'd been holding on to and clarity filled my mind.

Clarity and the question of what I wanted.

What I truly wanted.

I was always going to be a fashion designer. My love for that wasn't the same as wanting something. In my whole life I'd only ever truly wanted one thing and that was him.

Ryan O'Shea.

No one could tell me any different, and there wasn't a living soul that could stop me now.

Now, here, with him telling me that he found it hard not to touch me.

"Then touch me," I told him and it was as if the wall I'd placed up crumbled around me to welcome him.

I gazed up at him and savored the way his eyes darkened with desire.

"Touch... you." His gaze widened slightly then narrowed, like he wrestled with the idea.

"Touch me."

I moved closer to him and took his hand. His hand in mine was enough to awaken the magic that I only ever shared with this man. The boy I loved so much.

He stared down at my hand over his and his face etched with longing. He then smoothed his hand over mine so that it was him holding my hand, not the other way around.

He continued to look at our hands together. His light sun-kissed skin against the dark brown hue of mine was like art. The blend of color combined. Inspiration and creativity.

Everything we were. All that we ever were and still were.

When his gaze climbed back up to meet mine the desire came back into his eyes and passion swept through me, riding through my veins, heating my blood.

It raced through me when he stepped closer and I moved to him too. It was like a dance I knew the steps to.

He only released my hand to cup my face. I closed my eyes to relish his touch, the touch I'd longed for, for what seemed like forever.

How I used to dream of this.

He ran his fingers over the edge of my jaw and when I opened my eyes he lingered on my chin, tilting it upwards toward him.

"Lana…you still feel like my girl," he confessed.

He pulled away and gazed back at me with that pain again in his eyes. Pain and hurt that made guilt sweep through me in abundance.

"You still feel like mine too." The words straight from my heart felt like freedom. Like true freedom from what I'd run from.

The pain subsided when I moved back to him and as he lowered to my lips I welcomed him, wanting nothing more than him.

The man I'd lost.

He captured my lips and gave me an earth-shattering kiss that scorched me clean. The minute he did that all the reasons that had sent me fleeing from this town faded.

His mother threatening to destroy me, her telling me I wasn't good enough for her son and me believing it.

It all faded away, dissipating from my mind.

Fire swept through my soul the more he kissed me.

The kind of fire that spoke of what was to come.

Not like a prelude. It was more of a promise.

A promise my heart yearned for.

CHAPTER 12

LANA

HUNGRY WASN'T ENOUGH of a word to describe the intensity of the kiss.

It was however all I could think of as my blood sang through my veins and I craved more.

More of him.

He pulled me flush against him, and angled my face so he could deepen the kiss. When his tongue swept over mine and reached into the recesses of my mouth I knew within moments I'd be lost.

He moved over to the wall with me and pinned me against it with the hardness of his body. Hard and hot.

Equally hot fingers ran over my waist, tugging at my dress, bunching it up so much it rode up to my hips.

A desperate moan fell from my lips.

I had that out of body experience again because I couldn't believe how desperate I sounded. Desperate for the moment with this man I'd never thought I'd have again. Desperate to fight myself and the will that made me decide I could be without him. How foolish was I?

This was us.

How we used to be in the past. We were two people who were like combustible energy and passion.

We were the same people. Not that different at all, just older and clearly wanting each other with the same passion that had filled our younger selves.

When his lips moved from mine and trailed down my neck, my knees buckled. He moved back just a little to look at me in that fascinated way he used to. I'd never bothered to hide the effect he had on me then and it was useless now. Only one man had been able to weaken my body like that and it was him.

I reached back for him and tugged on his shirt, pulling him back to me.

"Don't stop touching me," I told him. It sounded like a plea. It was. Part of my desperation, part of my need to have him.

"Like fuck, I don't plan to stop." He promised with

that badass easy grin that always melted me, and in the same breath moved the little straps that held up my dress down my shoulders.

Like a puppet on a string I allowed him to do whatever he wanted to me.

Desire, dark and dangerous, darkened the bright blue of his eyes to a deeper blue. Now reminding me of the last traces of the sky before night took over.

My dress floated down to my legs when he undid the zipper on the side. Then his gaze raked over my body followed by hot, lust filled invisible fingers that burned me everywhere his eyes touched.

He took a prolonged moment to look at me and a sudden awareness rushed through my mind at what he might think of me. I was eighteen the last time we were like this, and I looked different.

I was probably what people called the late bloomer. I didn't really get my full woman-sized body that I took such pride in until I was about twenty. That was what he looked at now, checking out all the changes to me.

He slid his fingers over the flat of my stomach, right over to the edge of my panties and hooked his fingers in between the lace.

"Black lace..." He breathed tugging on the edge, looking at me like he savored me.

Before he could go any further I reached for him again, pulling on the edge of his white t-shirt.

"You, I want to see you too."

He didn't need to be told twice. He pulled the t-shirt over his head and whipped it off, unleashing the masterpiece of a body he had underneath. My lips parted as I stared. I wasn't the only one who'd changed. He had too.

Teenaged Ryan was the stuff dreams were made of, but thirty-six old Ryan was a fantasy.

Hard muscle lined the length of his abs. Hard, deep muscle that was separated into peaks and valleys. Peaks and valleys that were inked with more tattoos than when I last saw him like this.

Seventeen years ago he just had the Japanese character for fire on the edge of his hip. Now he had a few more characters and I loved that he'd had them done in such a tasteful way so as not to take away the attention from the rest of his body. The rest of him that I wanted to relish and run my fingers over.

I touched him, running my palms over his chest and down to his happy trail, stopping by his belt buckle and gazing down at the distinct bulge of his cock pressing against the front of his Levi's.

It was only when he cupped my breasts that I looked up.

Lightly, he ran his fingers over the already diamond-hard peaks of my nipples then with one quick snap, undid the clasp holding my bra together.

As the bra drifted down my shoulders my breasts spilled out, puckered and full as they bobbled toward him.

He took charge again, pinning me up against the wall. I moaned into the mindless pleasure that gripped my being when he bent low and took my left nipple deep into his mouth. Deep, deep, taking the nipple and as much of the flesh as could fit. The sight of him sucking was so hot I became wet in an instant.

He circled his tongue over my nipple and lapped at the tip making it diamond-hard with an aching need I felt straight in the pit of my core. He then sucked hard like he could truly taste me, the luxurious sensation curled my toes and awakened the raging arousal I'd always had for him.

I lost my mind when he started alternating from one breast to the other, giving each the same attention.

Sucking, licking, lapping, tasting.

All like he wanted to devour me whole.

He moved back again with a wicked smile when he saw what he was doing to me, making me come undone against the wall in his arms when we really hadn't gotten going yet. This was just the start.

Ryan moved back to my stomach and placed hot fiery kisses over the flat plane and tugged at the edge of my panties with his teeth.

I gasped and he gave me a deep chuckle. He then

nuzzled his face between my thighs and ran his tongue over the lace covering my mound.

I watched him, getting sucked into the wildness of him when he rolled my panties down my legs and that smile came back to his handsome face accompanied by the sin that glittered in his eyes.

Before I could catch my next breath he went back to my mound, now licking over my bare skin. One thrust of his tongue straight into my pussy and I gasped, grasping onto his wide shoulders.

He moved my thighs apart and thrust deeper, his tongue pushing past my folds and sweeping over the already sensitive hard nub of my clit.

"*Fuck*... Lana. You taste so damn good." He spoke in a rough voice, husky with sex.

I couldn't answer. The passion that cascaded over my body held me there in its grasp and at his will.

The moan that fell from my lips when he pushed his finger deep inside me was answer enough. Answer enough for him to continue to keep doing what he was doing to me.

The beginning of a greedy orgasm coiled within me when he started moving his finger in and out of my core. As he sped up and started finger fucking me I thought I was going to faint from the pleasure.

Faster and faster he went until it became too much and I arched my back into the wall, tossing my head back as a greedy orgasm tore through me, my hair falling backwards then forwards over my face.

I writhed against his fingers and he went back to my core to drink the flow that came from me, taking in everything as if I were some rare, exotic dish. He licked and continued to suck, flicking his tongue over my clit as he did so.

The desire that filled his eyes aroused me all over again.

He stood up and the bulge against his pants was bigger. He reached for me and kissed me hard, squeezing and kneading my breasts. It pushed me over the edge of reality.

"For fuck's sake Lana, please tell me you're on the pill. I'm clean." He growled against my lips. "I want to be inside you, no barriers."

Nothing sounded better than that.

"Yes. I want you inside me. I want to feel you." My voice was heavy with the desperation that filled my soul.

Gripped with scandalous pleasure I watched, never taking my eyes off him for a second as he undid his belt buckle and shoved his pants and his boxers down his legs at the same time.

I could have been eighteen again. Because only a teenage girl could gawk at the length of his massive cock the way I was. Massive and erect, ready to be inside me.

Unlike that teenage girl I was back then who didn't know what the hell I was doing, I stepped forward and gripped the base. He smiled with pure satisfaction and clamped a hand down on mine when I started to move my fingers up and down the thick length of his shaft.

"Don't you want me to taste you too?" I asked, rubbing harder. He allowed me to continue stroking him for a few seconds until his cock strained up toward me.

"Later." He groaned. "Princess look at my dick, I won't last two seconds if you continue to do that."

I would take two seconds if that was what we had. Anything that saw me with him like this.

He took hold of me, picking me up so I could wrap my legs around his waist.

I held onto his shoulders and sucked in a sharp breath as he eased me down on to his cock.

The skin to skin contact made my body spasm with wild passion and ecstasy.

I was ready for him, always ready for him.

One thrust and he shoved deep inside me. The connection was so powerful and overwhelming we both crashed against the wall, moaning and groaning.

Liquid fire streamed through my body as he started to move inside me.

At first it was a slow grind then it sped up to a rhythm we both enjoyed. Moving together, perfectly giving and taking.

Then the tension of the pleasure coiled deep inside me and he sped up.

Pinning me harder against the wall he increased his pace and the smooth strokes of his pumps and thrusts became harder. Filled with need and greed.

Raw, primal greed and need that crippled my body with pleasure. Intense, insane wild.

And with that same rawness he started fucking me, fucking me hard until another orgasm took me, powerful and sharp like a blade that split me in two and severed me from reality. It left me weak and drained, crippled from the intensity.

But… he wasn't finished with me yet.

He pulled out of me only briefly. Just to set me down and turn me to face the wall.

My hands pressed against the cold concrete and my hair fell forward over my face.

I glanced behind me just as he gripped my hips and ran his hands over my ass.

"This is mine, all of you is mine." He spoke the way he used to, demanding, and there was no other route other than to obey because I wanted him too.

My gaze snapped around when he plunged back inside me and I cried out from the mindless pleasure.

This position was a hundred times more effective than the last. I felt every move inside me and it sent a sizzling wave of blistering pleasure through my soul.

He didn't hold back. Rough hard strokes rocked my body as his cock seared into me over and over again. It made my entire being shiver in contentment and splintered my mind.

The world would fade and come back again, then fade and faze out leaving us in this purely erotic moment which actually felt like the only time we were together that was truly ours.

First we were a secret sneaking around so our parents wouldn't find out about us getting up to no good in the house. He'd worried about what my mom would think. Never what his parents would think. Always my mom.

Then he wanted to show me off to the world and it never happened. It was like we never happened.

Pleasure rocked me again. *Fierce.* Then an orgasm hit me full force and sent me over that edge, leaving me open to all the emotions I'd ever felt with this man.

With our bodies burning, and the wild sexual sounds of our skin slapping together, we came as one.

Every inch of my body was alive with savage energy, every secret part of me crying out his name.

That was what Ryan O'Shea did to me.

His pumps slowed to a stop and he pulled me close to his chest, holding me.

I rested my head back against him burying my face in the side of his neck.

We didn't talk, we just stayed there like that.

Him holding me, reminding me of what I'd lost.

Resounding to me that I'd only ever feel like this with him.

He stayed the night and the thought played through my mind the whole time. Embedding itself in my mind as he took me again and again, and all over again.

My heart came alive each time. Then… it sunk into despair when I opened my eyes the next morning and found that he'd left.

CHAPTER 13

RYAN

EIGHTEEN YEARS AGO...

There were some things in life you did and you knew you'd either get in trouble for it or end up doing some damage.

Those were the things that interested me the most.

I knew right from wrong.

I knew that ninety percent of the time I was an asshole and yet I still did whatever the hell I wanted to.

The only thing that scared the absolute shit out of me was Amelia catching me with her daughter.

Me, who she knew had gotten up to all manner of shit.

There was no way she would have approved of me. She might even leave, quit or something like that and then she'd take Lana. Truth be told that was the very thing I would do if I'd caught my daughter with a guy like me.

For a person who claimed to be so smart, and for a person who actually was smart, I made a lot of dumb decisions.

That included my current state.

Me in Lana's room at twenty to midnight. Twenty minutes before I had to confirm my acceptance to Georgetown. Me with Lana in my lap with her legs wrapped around me as I devoured her lips.

Yes, I'd lost my mind.

It was all my fault though. All of it.

The story actually began like this. I met her when I was nine.

To the world it looked like we were enemies, or rather I was her enemy.

Lana didn't have a bad bone in her body and she never hated me, when she should have.

Not when I teased then bullied her constantly and

not when she saw me getting up to all kinds of shit with other girls.

All the while she fascinated me. Right from that first day when her mother came to work for my family. I laid my eyes on the little brown skinned girl with her hair braided into two cornrows, lilac ribbons were at the end of the long braids that fell down past her waist.

She looked like a doll. Literally like a doll with her large brown eyes surrounded by thick lashes and that pretty little mouth.

Over the years the doll like look only enhanced to what I called true beauty. The kind you couldn't replicate. That she was possibly the purest being I'd ever known in my life was another reason why a devil like me should have stayed away from her.

It was that kiss.

The kiss that happened months ago in the attic.

The kiss broke down the barriers I'd placed up for the last nine years of our lives because it gave me that taste.

A taste of her. That taste I'd always fantasized about. That taste that drove me insane from the desire that coursed through my body when my lips touched hers.

It made me want her.

More.

Anyone would ask the obvious question of why I'd

been such an ass to her all our lives and my answer would be this: I don't know.

I'd be the coward and lean on the side of the age old explanation of why guys bullied girls they liked.

One thing I wouldn't do was deny I liked her.

I may even be bold enough and take one step further to admit that I felt she was too good for me, and the knowledge of that enraged me. It fueled me with anger because I wanted something I shouldn't have.

I went with the easy girls, and the asshole I was savored the look of jealousy I'd see in her eyes whenever she saw me.

Anything to instill some response from her.

I was eighteen years old and I should have known better. I should have known much better on all fronts and as much as I liked her, a lot of what I'd done was no way to treat anyone.

As she kissed me back now with the same passion I gave her, temptation coursed through my veins.

The same temptation that made me sneak in here over an hour ago. The same temptation that made me sneak her out of class at school and lure her into my car.

We'd left the school grounds and parked up in the back of an alley where we made out for hours.

Fuck. I was a senior so I was allowed off campus, but she would have gotten in trouble if we'd been found.

She would have gotten in trouble anyway because I made her take her top off so I could suck her breasts.

We could have both landed our asses in trouble whether at school or with the police. I knew that but I didn't care.

The same temptation got me now, enticing me to take her virginity.

It would be so easy to do.

I'd been sneaking in here at night because her room was at the corner of the house on the east wing. While Amelia's room was on the northern side of the house, Lana basically had the top section to herself. Downstairs was the kitchen.

I could almost say with certainty that no one would hear us in here if I did it, but sometimes people did go in the kitchen late at night. If that happened there was a chance they could hear.

My damn dick was practically bursting to be inside her, aching to flow my load in her virgin passage, aching to claim her and dirty her up.

I wanted to. She wanted to. What stopped me from doing it was the part of me that must have had some good. That part inside me that thought I needed to do some more changing before I took the most precious thing she had.

Couldn't get that back once she gave it to me, and I

didn't want her to regret it. I'd lost mine years ago and it wasn't with anyone I wanted to remember.

Things like that never mattered to me, but I knew it would to her.

Twenty minutes to midnight, probably fifteen now and we'd just been kissing like we had earlier.

Five more minutes then I'd go and make the decision to go to college and study law or not.

Five more minutes of the wild beauty on my lap and I'd go.

Her beautiful silky hair slinked to the side so it hung partly over her face and her right shoulder.

She'd curled the ends so it hung in long graceful waves. After the wild make out session it was all ruffled and she looked like an erotic version of a mermaid in a dark fantasy.

Her tongue tangled with mine and while I knew I wouldn't give in to temptation and claim her, there were other things I knew we could do to fill the need.

I pulled away from her lips so I could look at her and that worried look filled her eyes.

She looked like she was always waiting for me to change my mind. It wasn't surprising since we didn't exactly do much talking these days.

I smoothed my hands over her breasts and gave them a good feel. The first time she allowed me to feel her up was at one of those stupid dinner parties Mom organized where everyone came.

It was a week after Lana had sent her application to Parsons. She'd heard back and was so happy. That asshole Barney started teasing her at the party, like he did every time and I answered him with a fist in his face when he asked her if she'd wanted to taste his cock.

I surprised the group when I took her hand and led her away to the garage. That was where I kissed her for the third time and took things up a notch.

Barney knew better than to mess with her after that. That motherfucker stayed right away from her because he knew that punch was a warning sign that I'd mess him up if I caught him looking at her the wrong way.

The worry faded from her eyes as I ran my fingers over her little nipples, through the cotton tank top. She'd been dressed for bed when I came in so she wasn't wearing a bra.

"Take your clothes off for me, princess," I told her. I wished I could have sounded less like I was demanding her to do it. It was that need that was speaking.

"What about Georgetown?" she asked in that meek voice.

I gave her a crude smile. "Ten more minutes princess."

Ten minutes.

When I looked at her pouty mouth I couldn't help myself.

We both knew how I felt about Georgetown, and everyone knew how I felt about going to college to study something I didn't want to do. It didn't exactly help that I'd gotten into twenty off-the-charts amazing colleges, and that had been me just doing my best. I went into my SAT's without a day's study and got the best score in the school, which was sixteen hundred.

"Take your clothes off," I repeated and squeezed her left nipple between my thumb and forefinger.

"Okay." Nervously she slipped off my lap and took the hem of her top first. She pulled it over her head unleashing her perky tits.

My damn mouth watered and my dick hardened as if it were the first time I'd seen her naked, or fuck, like it was the first time I'd seen a girl naked. She'd just managed to make me crazy. Crazier.

Her breasts bobbled as she lowered to take off her pants and it was clear she was nervous but doing this for me.

She stepped out of the pants and her hands started shaking when she tugged on her panties to take them off. I was so damn fascinated with how beautiful she was that I sat there dumbfounded and stunned. Not oblivious to how nervous and uncomfortable she was, but allowing stupid curiosity to take control of my mind as I watched her.

I was nearly drooling when I saw a little peak of flesh on her mound, just like last night and I knew that as much as I told her to take her clothes off and I meant all of it, there would be no way I'd be leaving this room tonight and I'd be screwed.

Mom would kill me if I didn't agree to accept the offer from the one college she'd dreamed of me going to since birth.

Also, if I stayed for longer than ten minutes, and it was maybe eight or nine minutes now, I really would lose control and Lana would lose that virginity of hers I'd been so careful with.

I caught her hands, stopping her from going further and slipped my hand around her tiny waist to bring her to me.

Dainty hands pressed against my chest and she held my gaze. When she looked at me like that it felt like she was staring into my soul. It was the same look she'd given me a lot over the years. It was the sort that showed she was looking for the real me, and whatever she saw in me made her look past the asshole I'd been.

She closed her eyes when I moved to her neck and kissed her between the elegant crook.

I nibbled, sucking on the soft flesh just enough so it wouldn't leave a mark. Of course I filled my palms with her gorgeous breasts while I did so, torturing myself as I felt her nipples harden beneath my fingertips. Her bare skin in my hands warmed, heating up the more I touched her. Heating up and hardening.

I trailed a line of kisses from her neck straight down to her right breast and moved my hand over so I could suck.

Torture was a mild version of what I was doing to myself and I was practically pitching a tent by the time I moved to her left breast and started feasting.

Two minutes and I'd stop. Two minutes and I'd go. I couldn't stay any longer. A little moan fell from her lips and the light flutter of her fingers over the bulge

of my cock made me suck harder. When she gripped my shaft through my Levi's and started rubbing up and down I stopped and pulled away.

"Enough, I gotta go," I said, standing up. Or more like bolting upright like I'd been jolted with a zap of electricity.

The ache between my legs was too much and I'd sooner run away like a coward than embarrass myself in front of her.

Her brows knit together and she grabbed her tank top, shrugging back into it. I could see she was annoyed but I didn't have time to deal with that. I reached for my jacket and headed to the door.

"Why don't you want to sleep with me?" Her voice

pierced into me and I stopped short, my hand hovering over the door handle.

I turned back to face her, she was just pulling her pants back on.

"We've been doing this … *thing* for months. This thing, whatever it is. It's a game isn't it? To make me feel more like shit. You know how I feel about you and that's the part that's funny. That's the part that's a joke because it's *me*. Maid Girl."

As I looked at her and saw the pain fill her eyes, no torture on earth, or fear of embarrassment could send me through that door. She was right, she was absolutely right.

We were physical but I hadn't exactly changed. Physical was just physical. It left you with assumptions.

"No," I answered.

She continued to survey me and I felt worse when the hurt in her eyes deepened.

"I saw you with her today. *Tiffany.* You were with Tiffany. You went down to the old changing rooms. The funny thing was that at lunch time, before we left campus, I promised myself I'd never allow you to touch me again, and look at the day we've had." A tear ran down her cheek.

It moved me back to her. It moved me right back to her to cup her face. Her beautiful, beautiful face.

"I didn't do anything with Tiffany." I shook my head.

She grimaced. "Ryan. Do you seriously expect me to believe that? God knows what you haven't done with her."

"Not today." I wouldn't deny what I'd gotten up to with Tiffany. No, I wouldn't and telling her what I did do with Tiffany today would show more of how I felt about Lana than I was ready to admit. But fucking hell, I was listening up well to what she was saying and I knew if I didn't cough up the whole truth I'd either lose her or she'd actually start to hate me. "She wanted to talk to me because I haven't been with her in months. I told her I couldn't be with her anymore."

Lana's eyes widened slightly. "You told her that?"

"I did."

That was the short version of what happened. The vicious Tiffany knew I was seeing Lana. In fact I was pretty certain a number of people had guessed at school. It was just at home where it was a secret.

Tiffany knew I was seeing Lana and lashed out at me, asking me how I could ditch her for my maid's daughter, and if I didn't realize who she was.

Like fuck, as if that mattered. Her father owned a property development company and they were incredibly wealthy. So was I, and wealth didn't mean shit to me.

"What does that mean?" she asked. Her voice was faint.

I stared at her, really looking at her and thought about my answer. "It means I'm with you. *But…*" I pressed my hand to the flat of her stomach and slid down to the edge of her waist. "It means you give yourself to me when I deserve it. When you're sure it's me you want to be with."

She looked genuinely shocked and another tear ran down her cheek. "I want to be with you Ryan O'Shea."

I wanted to ask why.

Why of all the people would she choose me. She could do better. I knew it, I just wasn't sure she knew it.

I smiled and thought I'd bring back some lightheartedness to the conversation.

"That's going to take more than five minutes even with the tent I'm pitching," I joked. When she gave me a little smile I secretly rejoiced because I knew I'd got her back. "And, not here."

"Where?"

I bent down to kiss her. "I'll think of somewhere special." That seemed to make her happier. "I'd better go before I turn my future upside down."

"Okay."

"See you in the morning."

One last kiss and I left her.

I went down the back stairs that would lead to the corridor outside the kitchen.

I loved this house for many things, this was one of them.

All the back stairs and secret passages were an asset to a guy like me.

Excellent for getting in and out of my girl's room.

My girl....

God, it was the first time that I'd ever thought of a girl as mine. It felt though like she always was.

I was about to proceed past the library when a shadowy figure made me stop.

Someone else was down here in the back corridor.

Who was it?

The figure moved into the light that shone from the library and I saw it was Mom. She wore her dressing gown that flowed about her as she strolled down the pathway and stopped by the largest pillar.

I hung back in the shadows of the pillars near me so she wouldn't see me. She was looking at something and whatever it was she really didn't look happy about it.

From where I was I could get close to the library and see inside, so I did.

What I saw was Dad and Amelia.

Okay, nothing strange there.

Except...

Except maybe the circumstances. I glanced at my watch and saw it was now five minutes to midnight.

What were they doing together in the library at this hour?

Amelia as always looked beautiful. It was evident where Lana got her looks from.

To the casual passerby they looked like they were just sorting through some books. Dad handed her a small old-looking book and she smiled.

"Browning. I love this. His poetry always spoke to me," Amelia bubbled.

If I thought nothing of seeing them together before I would have corrected myself right about now. Dad gazed back at her and it was the way he looked at her that got my attention.

The admiration in his eyes said everything and piqued my suspicion, sending it through the roof.

To add to the look, he reached out and cupped her face briefly.

"You're the duchess. Proud and beautiful," he told her. I'd never heard him talk like that and he sure as shit never talked to Mom like that.

"Oh Connor, you shouldn't say such things to me." Amelia glanced down at the stack of books in front of them, bashful.

"Why not? It's true. You should have someone who can tell you that every day."

When she looked back to him I saw the same admiration. Even from where I was, I could see it.

Dad moved his hand away from her cheek. "You keep that. It belonged to my great grandfather."

"You can't give this to me." She shook her head.

"I just did."

There was a prolonged moment that held an air of anticipation when they just stared at each other.

"Thank you, Connor. Good night." She leaned to him and gave him a chaste kiss on the edge of his cheek then left, walking through the large oak doors at the furthest end of the room.

Dad stared after her.

I glanced over at Mom. She was still watching. She was still watching and I knew what she was thinking because I thought it too.

Were they having an affair?

Dad wasn't that kind of guy. He wouldn't do that. Look at him, the man read poetry and talked about duchesses.

Mom hated all that stuff. Amelia seemed to like it and they looked close.

I glanced down at my watch and frowned.

Two minutes to midnight.

I didn't have time to figure out whatever was going on.

I decided it looked innocent enough to me, even though Mom might think differently.

I had my own problems.

CHAPTER 14

RYAN

PRESENT DAY ...

I had my own problems to deal with and enough on my plate.

Why the hell did I always think it was a good idea to make things worse than they already were.

My focus right now should be Jack for a start.

I didn't see there being much of a problem in regards to Tiffany allowing me to see him but I couldn't rely on that.

Things may be rosy now but it could turn. She was the type of woman who could switch on you and I needed to be ready to play dirty if the time came.

My second and third focus should be Mom and this investigation.

Three things, three things that I should have been able to manage.

But, oh no, I didn't just stir the proverbial pot last week when I decided to jump on a plane, fly to LA and see Lana. It was more like I opened Pandora's box and unleashed everything that was beyond my control.

Everything meaning one thing.

The girl. The girl who'd bamboozled me from the dawn of time.

The girl—*woman*— I'd spent the night with and lost myself in her and to her all over again.

As the sun rose this morning, reality crept back in and asked me what the fuck I was doing.

Why was I letting myself back in for heartbreak?

As soon as Detective Gracen wrapped up this investigation Lana would be back on that plane to L.A and back to her life as Lana D'Angelo. A life I wasn't a part of.

It didn't involve me and the only difference between when she left last time and when she'd be leaving now was I knew where she was going.

After the divorce and after all the shit I'd gone through with Tiffany, I just wanted to get my life back.

What I was doing wasn't the way.

I went into the office, *late*.

Dad greeted me with a folder filled with paperwork.

"This fax came through for you this morning," he said, handing me the files. "It's a new case, they specifically asked for you. The client thinks she might be sued for breaking and entering into her own workplace and stealing trade secrets."

I frowned. It sounded like a good case but I wasn't in the mood. "Dad, isn't that more of a Johnson case? He loves anything to do with trade secrets."

"I think he's swamped. You know the only person suitable enough to do these types of cases is you." Dad smiled. "Plus if she is sued there's the aspect of the breaking and entering you can cover. Are you okay Ryan?" Curiosity filled his eyes as he looked me over.

"I'm okay." I wasn't sure if he knew Lana was back in town and I wouldn't tell him. I didn't want to talk about her right now.

"Cool, so will you take the case?"

I'd never been able to tell him no and I wouldn't start now. "Of course. I'll go look over the files now and make contact with the client."

Dad rested a hand on my shoulder and smiled. "Appreciate you son."

"I know. Right back at you Dad."

"I'm about to go into a meeting with our Japanese clients, but call me if you need me."

"Sure."

I left him and went to my office. I didn't even bother with my usual coffee before I jumped into work. I'd found that when I was like this coffee made me jittery and snappy. I didn't want to feel like that if I had to talk to people on the phone.

About twenty minutes into looking through the paperwork there was a knock on my door. I frowned because I didn't know who it was.

Janice, my PA knew to call me if she needed anything and Dad too would have checked with me first before coming to see me.

My mind conjured up Tiffany coming by. In all the time we were married she never came to see me here. After the divorce was when she started making her presence and it enraged me to no end.

If it was her and she'd come with her bullshit from yesterday I'd ask her to leave. Work was work and I didn't want shit following me here. She knew what I wanted and I wasn't backing down.

I straightened up in my chair, trying to get rid of the funk that had taken me since leaving Lana's house.

"Come in." I called out.

The door swung open and I saw the person I least expected to see.

Lana stood by the door looking as beautiful as she had this morning when I left her bed. Asleep or awake her beauty rivalled the angels.

With her hair pulled back into a ponytail her high exotic cheekbones were on display. Cheekbones on her beautiful face that I'd spent hours committing to memory.

As I stared I had to wonder if she was real. I'd found myself asking that question a lot over the past week.

She came in and the door shut behind her.

I had to stand up and go to her. It was an involuntary action like my body was drawn to her.

She gazed up at me when I stopped a breath away.

"I came to see you," she breathed, eyes searching mine. "You left and I didn't know if that meant it was over."

Over...

Suddenly I had that feeling I experienced all those years ago when I was in her room back at my parents' house. When she asked me why I wouldn't sleep with her. She'd thought I was still screwing around with Tiffany.

The look in her eyes back then was enough to steer me toward the ultimatum that posed itself in front of me.

Say the wrong thing and lose her.

Lose her forever.

It was like that now, although the situation was different. I already knew what it was like to love her, what it was like to be with her completely and to the point where you knew there was no one else for you. For me.

Yesterday I'd held back, as I'd tried to describe the shit sham show of a marriage I'd had with Tiffany. Tiffany who she'd hated.

What a fucking mess.

Logic and reasoning screamed at me. It told me to get a grip.

Then I noticed the way her eyes brimmed with tears. In that moment desire and fascination stepped right back in and took over.

The powerful force of all that I'd felt for this woman shoved everything out of my path. Out of my mind, out of my sight. *Everything.*

Over?

She hit the nail with the hammer. A sledge hammer that sealed it right into the concrete of reality.

Was it over?

Over… that was the thing. We were never over, it never ended. It wasn't over then and it wasn't now.

Her lips parted again as she was about to say more

but I stopped her with a kiss. A kiss that unleashed what I'd thought I could hold back.

I captured and claimed that pretty mouth of hers and I didn't care about the fucking consequences that would follow.

I moved with her to the little sofa in the corner of the room.

Dad bought it for me thinking it gave the office a nice touch and I could use it to discuss stuff with my clients. As if the other chairs in the office were made for something else.

I had the perfect use for the little sofa today.

I absolutely did.

Lana and I tore at each other's clothes until they came off layer by layer and I had her gorgeous naked body pinned beneath mine on the sofa.

The door was only closed but not locked and I didn't care. I pitied anyone who would think it was a good idea to barge in.

She moaned as I covered her gorgeous nipples with my mouth. Maybe anyone thinking of coming in would hear us and it would be enough of a warning to stay away.

Don't come in at all.

Her lips returned to mine the second I came up for air and the ache in my cock to be inside her got the better of me. No more kissing and no time to explore. We would do that later.

Roughly, I flipped her around so I could take her from behind. My crazy mind took the agonizing second to admire her gorgeous ass and the deep arch in her back.

One look and I was a goner. There would be nothing slow about us today.

I gripped her hips and guided the fat head of my cock to the delicious pink lips of her pussy and slid right in giving into the desperation that made me lose control.

As I seared into her heated passage, the walls tightened painfully around my cock, feeling so good, yet so tight it was painful. She soon adjusted to take my width though, once I started to move.

I tried for a controlled pump but I lost the battle and my body took over. Emotions guided me and made me give into that raw, carnal need that possessed my being with ultimate pleasure.

Then I made the mistake of glancing over at the glass filing cabinet across from us and saw our reflection. Our truly, erotic, scandalous reflection showing me the picture of us in the mad lock of passion, giving into the call of desire.

Her on her knees moaning with her massive

caramel tipped globes bouncing with each pound I gave her. Me behind her beautiful body fucking her.

Us on the sofa of my office at work.

The sight of us and the thought sent me over the edge.

It sent me spinning over the cliff of logic and reality and I didn't want to go back.

I wanted this.

Whatever it was.

No matter how long I had it for, no matter what it would do to me. I wanted it. I wanted her.

As her orgasm took her and she cried out my name, it took me too. The tight walls of her pussy gripped me in the lock of the wild recklessness of us and I surrendered ... everything.

Everything...

We collapsed in a hot sweaty heap and as I slipped my hand around her waist she reached for it and laced her fingers through mine.

I moved closer to her ear and planted a kiss there.

I hoped I answered her question of whether or not we were over. To be clear about what I wanted and needed I had another idea.

"Get ready we're going." I told her.

She twisted her head around to face me. "Where?"

"Home."

CHAPTER 15

RYAN

LANA STRADDLED my waist with those long golden brown legs and loomed closer to me with a spoon filled with strawberry ice cream.

We'd already finished a tub together just like this, except I covered her breasts with the ice cream and strawberries and ate them off her.

She'd decided on more ice cream and I had to say there were no complaints from me. When we were kids we used to beg Amelia to let us have ice cream for dinner.

She did occasionally. Then a few times before I got

truly horrible, Lana and I would sneak downstairs and eat the ice cream Dad stocked for the parties. I used to threaten to cut off her Barbie doll's hair if she told anyone I was down there.

No way would I have guessed that this would be us in the future.

Us lying in bed.

Her on top of me with her gorgeous breasts before me bouncing with temptation as she moved and me lying here like some kind of king who had everything.

I took the ice cream as she placed the spoon to my mouth but a little bit fell onto my chest.

My girl knew exactly what to do. I saw the saucy look she gave me as she lowered to lick the ice cream from my skin.

"You taste good," she cooed.

"My chest couldn't possibly taste as good as yours," I teased, reaching for her little nipples.

"I think it does. But I know where tastes better than your chest." The lascivious smile on her face told me she had other plans for me. "I haven't tasted you properly this hour."

Wild seduction raced through my blood when she slid lower and secured a slender hand over the base of my cock.

Fucking hell. The woman was perfect. The perfect

goddess who'd had my body under her control for the last few days.

Yes… days.

We'd been at my house for days.

Seven days.

The fucking week.

Mostly in this bed, or up against the granite walls of my shower, or on the table in the kitchen.

All I knew was, we had food, water, and we were here.

I used the last shred of responsibility left in my mind to contact my PA to let her arrange a meeting with my new client for next week.

As for this week, I was going to be out of the office, and I didn't want anyone bothering me.

Lana slid her hand up and down my cock and it strained in her hands, hardening. She knew just the right moment to lower her gorgeous head and take me into her mouth.

I groaned as she did and struggled to control my release.

It was so damn hard and became harder as I watched her head bob up and down my shaft.

Shit. I wasn't going to last. The look in her eyes and the way she worked me told me that was what she intended. Me to come in her mouth.

Just looking at her was so fucking sexy I wasn't sure how I hadn't yet.

The sweet suction of her mouth overwhelmed me and my balls tightened painfully in response, making me growl from the intensity of pleasure that raced through me.

That just encouraged her to suck harder. My body tensed, blood pumping so hot in my veins it scorched me clean from the inside out.

I knew that was it, all I could handle. The climax built, rising on a crescendo of wild sexual heat as she pumped the base and my release came, exploding hot cum into her mouth which she took.

She took it and kept me there inside, taking every last drop.

As she licked the tip of my cock and smiled I gazed back at her unable to talk.

Me...

I couldn't believe this was me, or that that was her.

"Was that good?" she cajoled.

I wasn't sure what sort of question that was. It had to be of the rhetorical variety we'd laughed about the other day.

"You know it was."

Her sexy lips parted, ready to answer me with one of her replies that would probably throw me but the ring of my doorbell interrupted.

We both looked toward the door.

We were upstairs in bed and I wasn't expecting anyone.

"I don't know who that is?" I stated, shuffling to straighten up.

She slid off me and wrapped the sheet around her.

"Maybe it's important. Ryan we've been in this house for days, it's like we skipped out on the world." She laughed and it was the sweetest sound.

"That was the idea." I grinned.

I couldn't stop looking at her.

The woman was beautiful. She always was, but it wasn't just that, that made me stare. It was that inner beauty that came from her personality. That unique thing about her that always drew me to her.

When I heard the main house door opening from downstairs I knew exactly who it was.

"Shit." I gasped and reached for my jogging pants.

"Who is it?" Lana asked in a hushed voice.

"My dad. He's the only one with a key to this place. Shit."

While I pulled on one of my old college T-shirts, Lana grabbed my button-up work shirt from the floor and shoved it on.

"Ryan?" Dad called out from downstairs. There was a worried tone in his voice and the first thing I thought was: what if something happened to Mom?

"I'm gonna see him." I told Lana quickly and rushed down the stairs to meet Dad. He'd gone into the kitchen and was just coming out.

"Dad!" I beamed, on the edge of a ragged breath. Admittedly, my damn heart was still racing and I was still struggling to catch my breath after Lana's magical mouth on my cock.

Dad sighed with relief and the noticeable tension in his shoulders loosened when he saw me.

"Ryan! God. *Kid*, you could give an old man a heart attack. You don't answer your phone anymore?"

I never heard it ring. My parents had one number for me and everyone else had another. After I left Tiffany I got a new phone.

"Is everything okay?" I asked again, thinking about Mom.

He frowned. "No of course not. I came to see if you were still alive."

I tried to bite back a smile and failed. "I'm alive Dad and I'm sorry. I just lost track."

"Of the days?" He raised his salt and pepper brows, and the grey streaks at the side of his head raised too. "Ryan you've been out of the office for the whole week."

"I'm sorry. I was just having some down time."

"You okay? I wouldn't have come in the house like that but I was worried. I know you're more affected from seeing Lana than you're saying and I just wanted you to know that I'm here for you kid."

Oh boy did I ever feel guilty.

Dad didn't need to tell me he was there for me, or that he worried over me. He'd carried the same worried look for the last seventeen years.

Worry and grief.

Worry for me. Grief for Amelia and Lana. The least I could have done was told him she was back in town.

Or in my house.

"Thank you Dad."

"Son, I feel the angst and the tension, so please talk to me. I admit I thought she would have come by now and I was hoping to see her. Personally, I'm just waiting for Detective Gracen to get back to me so I know I'm not needed here, then I'm flying out to L.A. to see her."

My nerves spiked. "Oh, Dad you don't have to do that."

"I'm doing it. I'm like a worried parent here. She was like my kid too. I've held off for the last six years giving her more space than I should. Hearing that her mother's investigation has been reopened must have done a number on her. I just need to see if she's okay."

The creak on the stairs cut him off from continuing.

Dad wouldn't have expected me to have company and definitely not a woman at my house. Not at this house.

So when Dad first glanced up the stairs I could tell he must have been thinking the creak was the house making noise. The steps on the staircase were wooden and had been known to creak every so often on their own, depending on the weather.

Dad did a double take and looked back up, keeping his focus there.

I looked too, but I already knew Lana was there.

She wore my shirt and that little skirt she'd worn here on Monday.

I could see she'd done her best to neaten up her hair but it still had that wild sex look. It hung to the side in waves.

I bit the inside of my lip when she glanced at me then looked back to Dad who was still staring, looking at her like he was trying to figure out if she was really there.

I knew the feeling.

I guess though that it was different for him. I didn't need to be told that Dad thought of her as his own.

"Lana?" Dad asked. I felt worse when his eyes glistened with tears. "Is that really you?"

She nodded and sucked in a sharp breath. "Yes...Mr. O'Shea."

I could see the emotion swelling in my father's face. It moved him to her and she moved to him, flying down the stairs straight into his arms.

It was strange, looking at them, she looked younger almost childlike. Like how she looked before she'd left.

"My dear girl." Dad gushed, holding her to him.

I really should have told him she was back.

He glanced at me and I half expected him to look at me like I should have told him, he didn't though.

The look in his eyes was of understanding.

There were a lot of things going on, or that had gone on, that no one was saying, not talking about at all, just going through the motions by themselves.

We just had to understand.

Like me still not knowing why Lana left.

However, this week wasn't about that. I knew too I was guilty of not telling her I got married to Tiffany, or the whole story of what happened to me in regards to Jack.

I would tell her though.

No matter what happened I would tell her.

It wasn't important when I first brought it up but it became important with the days that followed.

I couldn't blame Dad for wanting to catch up with Lana.

He looked so proud when she told him about her

work. They laughed about her little office back at the mansion in the attic, which was actually still there.

They laughed about a lot of things, but I noticed how surprised Lana was when she heard he'd looked for her. In her eyes was a mixture of sorrow and surprise. It was almost like she really never expected him to do that. I noticed too the tact Dad showed in the way he talked around everything but never asked why she'd left.

I'd hoped she would divulge something to him, but she was the same as she had been with me.

She gave an apology. An apology with no explanation.

It was the first time I'd decided to just accept it for what it was.

We had lunch together and it was almost like the kind of Sunday we'd spent together as a family, with the exception of Mom and Amelia being absent.

We ate in the garden enjoying the scenery. I'd gone back inside to put the plates in the dishwasher and when I came back out I heard Lana saying she should get going.

While I knew I couldn't keep her with me forever I was hoping she'd stay with me for one more night.

She stood and hugged Dad promising she'd see him soon then looked over at me as I approached. A tentative smile arched her pretty mouth when she saw the obvious crestfallen look on my face.

I was also very aware of Dad's keen eyes on us. He'd been like that the whole day.

"Hey." She smiled wider.

"Did you say you should get going?" I quirked a brow.

"Ryan I need clothes, and have you seen my hair?" She winced.

"You look perfect, and you actually don't..." My voice trailed off when I realized Dad could not only see us but we were in earshot of him. "You don't need anything," I stated. That was a much calmer version of what I was going to say.

She giggled. "I feel like a cavewoman, and I caught a glimpse of myself in the mirror and it confirmed I'm starting to look like one too."

"The mirror was lying, princess. But... I get it." I got it, I'd just turned into a poor sap who'd done a complete turnaround from wherever it was I was going to switching up my focus to her.

She reached out and touched my face.

"I'll see you for lunch tomorrow?"

I was already nodding before she could finish talking.

"I'll come get you." That meant a very short day at the office.

Her eyes gleamed with a sheen of purpose that reached out to me.

I didn't care that Dad was here, or that he was watching us, or that it must have looked like he'd walked in halfway through a movie and didn't know what was going on. He'd never known I was seeing her years ago and I always regretted that.

I always regretted that the person who I truly wanted to gain respect from was dead. I never got to tell Amelia how much her daughter meant to me.

Maybe she could see now. Maybe her spirit could see the emotion that coursed through my being.

I cupped Lana's face and lowered to give her a kiss.

Brief... but enough to say everything.

She blushed when I pulled away and waved to Dad. One last look and then she was gone.

I looked back to Dad when I could feel his gaze burning a hole in my back.

Curiosity wasn't a strong enough word to describe the look on his face.

I made my way back to him and sat down on the deck chair.

He eyed me up with that same curiosity waiting for me to talk, to give my rendition of what was going on.

"We... used to be..." I attempted and he inclined his head to the side.

He cleared his throat and ran a hand over his beard. *"Used to be?"*

I shrugged. "We were a couple way back when and then she left months after Amelia's death and I didn't know why."

Concern replaced the curiosity in his eyes. "Ryan..."

"Yeah. I know... I planned to drop out of college and be an artist. We were going to run away together, to New York. The day we were supposed to leave was the day she left. She never met me. I waited and looked for her everywhere, never found her until six years ago. You know the rest of the story."

Shock suffused his features, along with sadness.

It actually felt like a release of my soul to tell someone what happened to me.

"Son, I would never have imagined that's what happened," he sympathized.

"Yeah."

He shook his head. "Did she explain why she left or what happened?"

"No. I've tried to ask but she hasn't given me a straight answer. Just a bunch of stuff. She even said it was for the best."

Dad narrowed his eyes. "She wouldn't have just left you like that Ryan. It had to have been the grief. People behave differently and we can never know or truly understand what she must have gone through after her mother's death. Maybe we were a reminder. I don't know. What I do know without anyone telling me is she must have had a good reason to leave you." He lifted his shoulders and gave me a small smile. "I knew you were seeing her. Your mother and I both knew. What I don't know is why you never told us about her. God knows I would have been thrilled and my poor blood pressure would have had better years, or possibly stabilized, knowing you weren't hanging around girls like Tiffany."

Dad actually winced like he had a bad taste in his mouth.

"I know, then I had to go marry Tiffany."

"That was a disaster, but not something you should think about. You have Jack. Think of him. He's a beautiful boy who constantly looks up to you."

I nodded and thought I'd go back to answer the other part of his comment. "I didn't tell you about Lana because I'd spent so long trying to be the kind of guy I thought Amelia would want for her. If I told you, then she'd know. We were going to tell you all eventually. It was supposed to be New York first then we'd take it from there. I just... you guys knew what I was like. You knew how I treated Lana when we were younger. That's a lot of impressions to fix."

"I understand and I get it. I don't think Amelia would have been any different to me. She was her mother, she would have known the same as everyone that Lana had feelings for you from day one." Dad gave me a kind smile.

"You think so?"

"Know so. I remember the two kids who stared at each other when they first met. I recall the two kids who were probably doing their very best not to like each other and failing. I remember how she looked when she first saw you with Tiffany. I saw her look that way many times."

"I was an idiot."

"We can blame ourselves for a lot, but it's just how it played out. I truly wish I could have done more for her. I do. I felt like a failure more often than not in the last ten years. God knows what she went through when she left us. Amelia would have ..." Dad's voice trailed off and he stared out to the river.

I didn't know why but I recalled that night I saw him with Amelia in the library. I never really forgot that night for its weirdness.

I'd assumed nothing suspicious was going on between them but I always wondered.

It never stopped me from wondering if it might have. I never saw anything else to suggest it, but Dad always got this look in his eyes whenever Amelia was around. The grief that took him when she died was indescribable.

Hearing she'd jumped off the bridge, taking her own life was something neither of us would ever get over.

"She meant a lot to you didn't she?" I asked.

"Yeah. I just wanted to make sure she got that dream of hers to do fashion designing," Dad replied.

"Not Lana." I looked on at him in anticipation. "Amelia. I was talking about her."

His gaze clung to mine and he pressed his lips together. "Yes. She did. She... was like no other person I'd ever met. Extraordinary." There was that look again, and in reference to Amelia. It made me curious. "Do yourself a favor boy. Don't be afraid to do what you want to do. Don't try to please others. Don't think about what's right or wrong. Make sure you take care of you first. It's happiness in the end. I really wish like hell you'd gone to New York and become an artist. That is who you were supposed to be. Not the lawyer. Whatever you have with Lana now, explore it. Doesn't matter about anything else. She still looks at you the same way, and you her."

I released the breath I'd been holding on to as I listened to his words.

I definitely had to admit it was the first time in many years that I felt like myself again. I felt like I had hope, and it was because there was something I wanted.

Her.

CHAPTER 16

LANA

GEORGIE and I were still screaming with excitement over the phone.

We'd been on the phone for five minutes. The talking lasted for a few seconds just long enough for her to tell me she was pregnant. Then we screamed out the rest of the time.

God in heaven, I was so happy for her.

I was literally combusting with the excitement like it was me who was pregnant.

We were the same when she got married, but her engagement to Pat did not start out the way most

peoples' did. He was her boss/friend and their engagement was supposed to be fake.

I knew that was just a big fat eye-opener waiting to
happen because nobody on earth behaved the way
those two did, like they were already a couple. It took
the craziness of Pat to seal the deal.

Now they were going to be parents.

It was absolutely beautiful and the most wonderful
news I could hear right now.

"Oh Georgie," I gushed and a tear trickled down my
cheek. It snuck up on me but didn't surprise me. It was
the kind of news that brought tears of happiness to
your eyes. "Congratulations to both of you."

"Thank you my dear friend. I still can't believe it. It
doesn't quite feel real to me yet. It feels strange. But a
good strange." She laughed.

"I can just imagine. How did you find out?" We
hadn't gotten to that part yet and I was interested to
hear it all. I wished I'd been there with her so we could
scream properly.

"I thought I got sick from Pat's cooking. He made
me this elaborate dinner after I got back. And when I
say 'made', I mean he ordered it in and pretended he
made it. I saw the food cartons in the bin." She chuckled
and I rolled my eyes. That was just the sort of thing Pat
would do. He was crazy like that.

We both giggled and she continued. "Anyway I was

so sick and of course I thought it was food poisoning. The poor guy felt so bad because I couldn't keep anything down. I ended up spending the night in hospital and the next morning they told me the news. I'm four weeks pregnant."

I blew out a ragged breath. That all happened last week.

Last week when I was tangled in bed with Ryan.

God... I should tell her. I knew it was something she'd want to know and when the phone rang earlier it was something I'd wanted to talk about for certain.

It was something I needed to talk about because I didn't know what it was supposed to mean for me.

"Georgie, I'm thrilled. Sorry you were so sick you were in hospital though. Do you need me to come back?" I was serious. I would fly back in a heartbeat and see her, even for a day if she needed me.

"No, of course not."

"You know I would, and I will if you need me."

"I know girl. You don't have to do anything at the moment, especially with my crazy husband at my beck and call. He's decided to place me in a glass ball and laid down the law. I'm not allowed to move or go anywhere out of his range. He's hired a midwife and some other assistants."

I laughed. "That sounds good Georgie."

"He is over the top and you know who's worse? My

in laws. Lord have mercy. It's like all of us are pregnant. So sweetie, I'm well taken care of and I'm feeling heaps better. The doctors gave me some cool antacids so I can eat again." She sighed and the line sounded staticky. I'd noticed that a few times during the call. It was probably to do with the signal by the house.

She laughed and continued. "I'm more concerned about you. What's happening? We've been screaming for joy. I called a few times last week and I just thought you were busy. You said so in your text."

I texted a total of one time only and it was to tell her exactly as she'd said.

I said I was busy with stuff and would call her. I never got to though. The call of Ryan's masterpiece of a body was too much.

I placed my hand to my forehead and glanced over at the clock on the wall. He'd be here soon. It was ten to twelve.

Ryan would be here soon and I already knew what kind of day we were going to have. We were just like we had been as teenagers.

No... scratch that.

We were worse. We were worse than we were. The teenagers we were back then were actually a tamer version of the man and the woman who'd devoured each other all six ways to Sunday. Literally.

I had to shake my head free of the memory to focus.

"Yeah." I answered eventually with a little sigh.

"Anything happen with Detective Gracen? I guessed maybe nothing happened but did he make any kind of contact?"

"No, sadly not."

All of last week had passed and I didn't hear from Detective Gracen.

I knew these things took time but I was eager. Wrapped up in Ryan as I was, I was totally eager to hear if Detective Gracen had found anything out.

"Did... um, anything else happen?" she asked hesitantly. I knew my friend and the cautious tone her voice had taken meant she was referring to Ryan.

"Yes." I breathed.

I heard her suck in a sharp breath and I could almost visualize her sitting up straighter with that bounce in her hair.

"Like what? Lana sweet Jesus please don't keep a girl in suspense. I swear it's written somewhere that it's wickedness to get a pregnant lady all worked up, especially one who's your best friend. Something happened between you and Ryan, didn't it?" Her voice rose by several octaves.

"Yeah... it did."

"God, Lord, what? What happened? Did you sleep with him?"

My chest tightened and I tensed up. Saying it would make it all real.

"I did. We spent the week together."

She made a choking sound. "Oh my God. *The week!* Thank God I left and gave you the room to run free with the gorgeous man." She laughed out loud.

"Oh Georgie. I don't know what I'm doing." That was a confession of the truth enhanced and amplified with everything.

Everything including the knowledge that Mr. O'Shea had looked for me when I left.

Just knowing he cared that much meant more than I realized. Over the years I'd thought he was just like his wife. When Mrs. O'Shea threw me out I'd thought at the time that it was coming from both of them. In my wracked state of mind and body I didn't have the strength to decipher friend from foe.

The look in his eyes yesterday held the wealth of emotion that I'd always seen in him. It was the sort I'd always compared to that of a father.

I was in two minds about seeing him when he'd first arrived. Then I heard him say he was going to fly out to LA to see me and it was then that I knew he could have had no part in what his wife did to me.

"Lana, you're always telling me to follow my heart and live for the moment, seize opportunity and don't hold back. That's stuff you've said to me many times and I don't think I'd be where I am today if I never listened to you. When we met back in college, the first thing I'd noticed about you was your passion for what you wanted. I think you know what to do but you're holding back."

I nodded even though she couldn't see me. "Is there such a thing as telling yourself you're happy and believing it?"

"You know there is. I know for damn certain there's no way you could enjoy being busy the way you are all the time. No one can. You're gifted and talented and you've had the opportunity most people don't have by doing what you love for work. But there's a line. There's a line between working and enjoying what you're doing and becoming an over-obsessed workaholic who has no life."

I listened to her and wondered when it was she'd gotten so wise.

"You're right." I shuffled on the sofa so I could gaze out to the river through the floor to ceiling glass windows. "I wish that life could have been different. I wish that I could just tell Ryan what happened. I'm scared. It's not a nice thing to tell a guy who adores his mother that she hated his girlfriend so much she sent her away, and during a time that I needed people. I actually needed people around me."

It wouldn't just be telling Ryan, it was Mr. O'Shea too.

He'd deserved to know as much as Ryan did. Hearing he looked for me for two years showed that he'd done so with his wife most likely lying in the background and selling him some story of what might have happened to me.

"It's going to come out Lana. The truth has a way of coming out when it needs to."

Again, she was correct.

"Yes, I think that's what I'm afraid of."

"Don't be. Truth can do all sorts but it's a good thing."

Truth. It had a way of taking on a life force of its own and finding a way to reveal itself. Just like the past when Ryan and I first got together. When we did it felt like something that was waiting to happen. A long time coming.

Emotions brought out the truth.

Emotions drove you to your decisions. Mine had gone straight back to the girl I was so long ago. Over seventeen years ago who just wanted to be with the boy she loved.

The doorbell rang as if on cue to my thoughts.

It was the boy, now a man, and he really deserved answers, especially since I couldn't deny that I felt the same way I did about him.

"Sweetie, I'm so sorry. I'm gonna have to go. He's here." I didn't even register how that cut into our deep conversation.

"That's okay Lana. I'm glad he's there." There was a smile in her voice. "I'll come as soon as I can."

"You need to rest. How about I let you know if I need you to come? I have to take care of you now." I smiled.

"Okay, Miss boss lady."

"Congrats again. I'll call you later," I promised.

"You better." She chuckled and hung up.

I ran my hands over the soft cotton of my skirt. Nerves filled me, my nerve endings were tingling from yesterday when I got back and I couldn't stop thinking about Ryan.

I went to open the door and there he was looking like he'd just stepped out of the past.

He'd shaved and that automatically made him look younger. His clothes were what did it for me though. The black leather biker jacket, the white t-shirt that clung to his muscles, the Levi's hung low on his hips and the sexy way that lock of hair hung over his eye.

It took me a few seconds before I realized I was just staring at him, then he smiled, bringing out the dimples.

Before I could say hello his lips were on mine. Then

my clothes were off before I could take my next breath. His too.

In seconds we were both naked pressed against the wall of the living room, starting out the day exactly as I thought.

Me against the wall with him buried deep inside me.

Once we were finished in the living room, we ended up in my bed where we spent most of the afternoon.

I barely heard my phone ringing when it did and I was half tempted not to answer because Ryan was kissing my neck.

I only answered because I knew it could only be one of a few select people calling me. My first thought was Georgie.

But it wasn't Georgie on the phone. It was Detective Gracen.

"Hi Detective Gracen." I tried to sound bright but anxiety gave my voice a slight quiver.

"Hi Lana, I hope I haven't caught you at a bad time," he began.

"No, I'm fine to talk." I glanced at Ryan next to me in the bed who'd sat up the minute I'd said Detective Gracen's name.

"Good. I wonder if I could ask you to come down to the station as soon as you can. If you could come today that would be great. Tomorrow is fine though if this is too short notice."

His voice... there was something about his voice and the tone that lingered within it worried me.

"I can come now. I'll be there in half an hour tops."

"Perfect. Will your friend be coming with you?" he asked.

"No, she's not here."

"Oh, okay." The tone was there again.

Ryan had already slid off the bed and was dragging on his clothes.

"I'm going with you," he cut in with a determined nod.

I mouthed thank you to Ryan but a lump formed in my throat and I swallowed hard past it.

"Detective Gracen, I have someone coming with me. Can you give me an idea of what's happening? Did you get the results back, or find anything?" I doubted that he would be calling if he hadn't. I'd just figured that was the best way to ask the question of why he wanted to see me.

"We have," he answered and I realized the tenor in his voice was carefulness. That was what it was. "It's best if I see you in person. We'll talk when you get here."

"Okay. I'm on my way." My hands started shaking. Ryan noticed straight away and came to my side.

"Good. See you then."

Detective Gracen hung up.

I bit down so hard on my back teeth and the edge of my lip that I thought I'd pierce the skin.

"What did he say?"

"Not a lot. Ryan..."

He took hold of my shoulders. "Lana, let's go. Don't think too much or worry. We've all been waiting to hear what this guy has to say. Let's go see what's happening."

I nodded.

We got to the station in less than half an hour.

Ryan drove me which was great because I was too nervous to drive.

That lump in my throat was still there.

It was crazy though. Why was I so worked up? I already knew the worst had happened.

Mama was dead.

That was the end stage of what could possibly happen.

It wasn't as if she'd gone missing and I was waiting for the news of where she was or what had happened.

I already knew.

So, this was just details.

Detective Gracen came out to meet us in the foyer of the station and took us to his office.

"Thank you both for coming," he said, looking from Ryan to me, then back to Ryan. "I guess this involves you too Mr. O'Shea, so it's good you're here."

"What's happening?" Ryan asked.

"When we found the extra report document we did a full investigation on the lab it came from and looked over the findings it presented. The analysis has now come back and shows conflicting information to the report that was made in the final post mortem examination."

"What does that mean? Forgive my language, but that sounds suspicious as fuck." Ryan tensed. I knew that he only spoke like that when he was angry.

"It is. It *was*." Detective Gracen nodded. "It suggests tampering. We're still looking into that part."

Tampering?

My ears started ringing.

Why would anyone tamper with a report for a suicide victim?

Detective Gracen looked back to me, and his eyes filled with compassion. "We went with what the omitted report showed. The data listed on the report suggests that your mother was dead before she fell in the river."

My heart tightened up. It squeezed and my breath hitched. "She died before?"

He nodded. "Yes, we strongly believe that. There

were marks listed on her body conclusive to strangulation. Her windpipe was crushed and …" his voice trailed off when I wheezed.

Tears poured from my eyes. They just poured out like someone had knocked down a dam and the water had come crashing through.

I struggled for air to breathe. Ryan took me into his arms and it was only when he held me that I realized he was crying too.

"What are you telling us, Detective?" Ryan's voice cracked.

I was crying so much I could barely see. I didn't need the clarification.

I knew before he answered what he was going to say.

"We think she was murdered," he replied.

There it was.

The truth.

The answer. The truth…

Although… somehow I knew.

I didn't know *how* I knew, but I'd felt it. All this time I'd felt it.

I'd thought it all along in the pit of my stomach. Gut feeling, gut instinct.

That would have been the only way she would have left me without saying goodbye.

I screamed as it all hit me, as if my soul was weeping.

This was worse than hearing she'd died.

Knowing someone killed her.

My mother.

CHAPTER 17

LANA

I REMEMBERED the day we went to live with the O'Sheas.

The buildup was exciting because it meant that we'd be moving from that horrible apartment complex in Charlotte.

It was awful. The kind of place you couldn't feel comfortable in.

The sort of place that I, even as a child, knew to be wary of.

Situated on the outskirts of town, near the trailer park, the dinky apartment we'd lived in was all Mama could afford with her cleaning job.

Mama was supposed to be a teacher.

She'd taught English literature at the high school near the grade school I attended.

She'd loved that job so much and we were supposed to be saving to move somewhere nicer. It was all I'd hung onto and at nights we escaped in the world of fiction.

Mama loved poetry. She didn't think it mattered that I might have been too young to understand the words. She read poems to me.

She loved romanticism and the post-romantic era the most and she always read me something by Browning, Byron, or Swinburne.

I used to relish the sound of her voice when she'd recite her favorites to me.

Then she lost that job and she was so sad. She didn't tell me why, but I heard her talking to my aunt about it. They were arguing. They'd had a lot of arguments but this one was the worst. The principal found out that Aunt Larissa was not only a drug addict but she was dealing too. Mama lost her job because of that. Because of my aunt and her unsavory life.

The only thing Mama could do after that was clean. I always wondered why she never tried to go back to teaching but I never asked. She still read to me and as long as we had each other we had hope.

That hanging on to hope seemed to pay off when

she got the job at the O'Sheas. They needed a live-in housekeeper/nanny who could handle a large house and look after their son occasionally when they were working.

I thought *large house* was a complete understatement.

The place was more like a castle from the fairytales. There were other maids, a butler who wore a uniform, gardeners, someone to do this and someone to do that.

We were so excited for the chance to be there.

Most of all I remember thinking about how happy she looked.

She finally looked happy and that made me happy too.

It did throughout the years that we lived there. She was always working so hard.

Working so she could take care of me and working so she could take care of Aunt Larissa.

It wasn't until years later that I found out through another argument I overheard them having that she didn't go back to teaching because it didn't pay half as much as what she got at the O'Sheas. And, the only reason she took that job was because of Larissa. She worried about her drug problem and that one day something bad would happen to her little sister and she wouldn't be able to bail her out.

Look how it all turned out.

Aunt Larissa was wherever she was seventeen years ago, and someone killed my mother.

I was still trying to process that part.

Someone killed my mother.

All that beauty gone just like that. All that creativity, and love. She loved so willingly, so effortlessly. She was the most amazing woman I ever knew and I became who I am today because of her.

Someone killed her.

Who?

Someone killed my mother. Took her life. Killed her...

I sucked in an involuntary sharp breath. Maybe my body was reminding me to breathe.

Ryan took me home after our meeting with Detective Gracen and stayed with me.

I cried the whole time. I cried for hours after, crying out everything inside me.

It left me weak and completely drained out.

I'd made it as far as the sitting room where I stayed until the tears ran out, dried up like a desert. I felt the same too. Like all the life had been sucked out of me.

Ryan was mostly with me, then I remember him trying to call his Dad.

He'd held my hand, held me, did everything he thought I needed but nothing helped.

His warm hands over mine brought me out of my deep thoughts.

I focused my gaze on him. We were still in the sitting room. I was still sitting on the sofa. Still in the same spot.

The only difference was it was dark outside.

Ryan was holding a glass of water.

I was so caught up in distress that I couldn't remember him leaving my side to get it. It was like he'd just appeared before me.

Everything around me seemed to bleed into a blur. Time and movements around me, and my poor mind kept slipping back and forth between the past and present.

I gazed up at him with swollen eyes. His were red and he looked awful, just as bad as me.

"Try to drink this," he said, holding out the little glass to me.

I shook my head. I didn't want it. I didn't want anything.

He got down on his knees and held it out again.

"Princess… you have to drink something."

"No, I don't want it." Another hot tear rolled down my cheek followed by another. He set the glass down on the coffee table and took my hands into his.

"Lana, I'm so sorry. I'm so sorry that happened to

Amelia." He gulped hard and seemed to be holding back more tears.

"It's ...." I didn't know what to say. *It's not your fault, or thank you.*

Neither was right and I couldn't think straight.

"I don't get it Ryan. I just don't. You knew her, you knew what she was like, she never hurt anybody. She would never. Who would do something like that to her? Who would want to kill her?"

He bowed his head and the tears slipped down the side of his face.

"I keep asking myself that same thing ... it just doesn't feel real baby."

His grip tightened on my hands. "A part of me feels like I wish I didn't know. Better if I believed she took her own life than know someone took it."

He nodded. "I know. I'm trying to think how such a thing could have happened. I'm trying to think back to when it happened. We weren't there."

No, we weren't there at all. We were off on one of our little weekend getaways. Oblivious to everything and everyone. We didn't care about anyone besides ourselves and while I was with him someone killed Mama.

Words couldn't quite describe the agony that filled my soul.

Nothing could.

"Ryan what am I going to do? What am I really going to do?"

He got up and pulled me into his arms for the umpteenth time. "I'm here. Princess, I'm here with you. I don't care about the missing years, I'm here. We're going to do this together whatever we're supposed to do," he promised.

His words alleviated some of the burden that rested on my body. Some but not all.

There was still so much to process. It was the part I was avoiding thinking about. The part about the report being tampered with.

The doorbell rang and in my head it sounded like a gong echoing through my body. I knew it wasn't really that loud. To my fragile ears it was though.

"I think that's my dad. He said he was on his way," Ryan stated. I moved away from him so he could get up.

He answered the door and seconds later Mr. O'Shea came in looking exactly the way I expected him to look.

Tears blinding his eyes, face red and blotchy. He flew over to me, dropped to his knees in a similar fashion to the way Ryan had and took my hands.

"Lana…" he breathed. "I heard, I…"

All I could do was nod then more tears came and he held me. Deep sobs racked my insides once again. Once again it took me.

With that fatherly warmth he held me. "My sweet

girl, I promise you, we will get to the bottom of this. I promise you I'll find out who's responsible. I will find out. They won't get away with it."

His words were the words that echoed deep from inside me.

Finding who killed my mother was exactly my next step.

CHAPTER 18

RYAN

MOM WAS SITTING by the fire place in the sitting room watching the flicker of blaze from the wood. It cast a warm amber glow on her face.

Her thin gaunt face that looked thinner than yesterday morning when I stopped by.

I usually came to see her a couple of times a week. Because I was with Lana all of last week I'd missed seeing her so I was fitting in a visit in the morning just in case I didn't get to see her again until later in the week.

Yesterday, she'd seemed more vibrant. The color in

her face had returned and she almost seemed like her old self. Today, however, she bore a strong resemblance to when she was in the height of her illness.

That was in between her last few sessions of chemo and radiation therapy.

That was how she looked now.

Weak and frail. *Aged.* Like she'd aged another twenty years since yesterday.

I could see it on her face that she'd gotten a blow too, from hearing what really happened to Amelia.

I knew she would have wanted to run around as much as Dad had but was too weak to.

It wasn't cold at all but to her it was always cold. It was common in a lot of cancer patients who'd gone through chemotherapy to feel the changes in temperature a lot more than everyone else. That was one of the things the consultants had advised us on.

Mom looked to me as I approached and she brushed away a tear.

"Mom." I pulled up one of the chairs and sat next to her.

"Ryan... I'm completely numb." She nodded. "I'm so numb I can't do anything. I've been sitting here for hours. Since your father got back last night and told me what happened I've been like this. Could barely sleep. Can't eat."

I knew the feeling. "You must try to focus and rest

Mom. I understand how you feel but you need to think of you too."

I wouldn't know what I'd do if I lost her. I didn't know what I would do. She ran her hand through my hair the way she used to when I was a kid and I looked at her. She looked like a woman who'd gone through so much, and she had. Just looking at her was testament of that. Her hair had only just started growing back a month ago so she'd stopped wearing her scarf. Just looking at her hair ached my heart. I remembered the long golden locks she'd had when I was a kid and how everyone compared her to a Hollywood starlet for her beauty.

She would always be beautiful to me, no matter how she looked. The sickness however, was evident.

Her eyes looked tired. "You are always taking such great care of me." she cupped my face.

"I'm supposed to, Mom." I nodded. "Please try to rest. It won't be good if you don't. Dad and I will work with the police and get down to the bottom of what happened. We will try. We will absolutely try."

"I know you will. It's all just so sad. So very sad to know that happened to a woman who was practically family to me. She was like the sister I never had. The only person I would allow to take care of you because I trusted her. I can't quite express how I feel. When I thought she'd killed herself I thought ... God, Ryan...I wished I could have saved her. I wished I could have done anything to let her know she was loved and she didn't have to die. It didn't have to be that way. Hearing this, the truth …. Oh Ryan… I just can't." She brushed away more tears.

I was holding back again, holding back because yesterday when I broke down it was shock that got me. I only snapped out of it for Lana but the shock was still there.

"Mom, I know. I *know*. We'll get to the bottom of this." I promised. I meant it too. Not just for her sake. For Lana.

For Amelia.

There was so much at work here, so much to be addressed.

Even though Detective Gracen stated that they didn't have solid proof as yet I knew he was just saying that out of formality to cover himself in case of not finding proof.

I knew the damn ropes.

He'd told us what he told us because he could. He wouldn't have said all of that if they weren't at least ninety percent certain. It was what suspicion pointed to.

So here was my theory. Someone killed Amelia. Someone powerful enough to screw with evidence and reports but obviously not clever enough to make sure all traces disappeared. Or they just didn't think that far ahead, or whoever they paid off in the coroner's office hadn't done a good enough job.

Fuck. It was all so unreal. So this person created the whole thing to make it look like she committed suicide.

That was the essence of what happened.

Why?

That was what I wanted to find out. I figured if I got that part it may lead me to something else. I needed a motive. I'd thought of Amelia's sister Larissa because even I knew what went down with her many times with her history of drugs.

Larissa lived in a dangerous world. It was reasonable to think that maybe someone to do with her got to Amelia. People like that had a lot of power. I'd seen it.

Someone entered the room from behind us. When I turned around my heart sank right into the ground when my gaze landed on Tiffany standing in the doorway.

What the fuck was she doing here?

I couldn't resist the frown that automatically formed on my face. It was an automatic response to seeing her. Mom on the other hand was all smiles. It was as if someone had sprinkled magic dust on her head and wiped away our prior emotional discussion.

She'd always liked Tiffany. It was strange to see the

difference in reactions from my parents. Dad couldn't stand her, never could.

"Hi." Tiffany beamed, coming closer. She walked right up to Mom and gave her a kiss on her cheek.

I had to wonder what the hell it was she was playing at because she rarely visited my parents when we were together. Why had she started now?

My visit today was impromptu so she wouldn't have known I'd be here. That would have been suspicious. *More suspicious.*

"How nice to see you my dear," Mom cooed.

"You too Kathy. I thought you might want some company for lunch."

"You always were such a dear. I'd love the company. You can join Ryan and me."

"I won't be staying," I cut in.

Mom gave me a hard look. "Ryan, please. It's the simple things that help during times like this."

I didn't get it.

I really didn't get how she could be so accepting of a woman who lied about something so big as our child not being mine.

I didn't understand it.

Mom claimed that Tiffany was scared and she'd been completely against the divorce. Never thought about the whole context that happened. That Tiffany basically set a trap for me and I landed straight in it like it was a fucking spider web.

It was Mom who advised me to marry her when Tiffany found out she was pregnant. Maybe if she didn't I would have made some arrangement.

"I'll be going in a minute," I told her. That was actually the truth. I'd just come to see how she was. Tiffany's arrival only accelerated my departure.

Tiffany looked my way and gave me one of her stiff smiles. Stiff from the fakeness and stiff from whatever shit she'd pumped in her forehead with this month's maintenance money she'd gotten from me.

I was in no mood for shit today so I didn't even bother to acknowledge her.

"I'm gonna go check to see if lunch is ready," Tiffany stated, and left us.

Mom was already looking at me with that disapproving stare.

"Ryan I really wish you would just forgive her. You guys have such a beautiful family. Yes she made a mistake and I would be hurt too, but we make mistakes. She was perfect for you."

I gave her an incredulous glare. "No. Mom she wasn't perfect for me. She wasn't anything for me. Not her. Never her."

"Ryan dear, I hear that Lana has made her grand

return. I sincerely hope she hasn't swayed your thoughts."

So… this was what it would be like to talk to my mother about Lana.

"She has not. Whatever happens between Lana and me has nothing to do with Tiffany."

Her gaze hardened right up and actually stunned me. "Ryan, you are my son and naturally I want the best for you. You talk like you're with her. If you are, I implore you to think. Think long and hard. That girl left us without a word of where she went. She just left. Look how we cared for her and she just left. Once this investigation is over what do you think she'll be doing again? *Leaving.* That's what. She will not care about you. Tiffany has always been in your life. She was the girl who was the constant." She nodded like she truly believed that.

Her words about Lana got to me though. She was mostly right. Lana would leave after the investigation. That was a given, it was expected. I knew that would happen in the grand scheme of things.

However it wasn't important now.

I leaned forward and took her hand.

"Mother." I only ever called her that when I had something important to say. "I love you. I love you like nothing else and I value you. I've done a lot of things in my life that I didn't want to do but I did them to make you happy. There are however, some things I don't think you have a say on. Tiffany is one of them."

"Ryan, it would make me so happy to see you two together again."

I shook my head and geared up to tell her the one word she'd rarely heard from me.

"No," I said.

I said the word, and it felt like a step in the right direction.

I'd always had a very difficult time telling her no. It wasn't something she was used to hearing from me so hearing it now stunned her. "I'm really sorry. But no. I'm gonna focus on this investigation and then get my life back on track. She is not included in my plans for that."

"And Lana is?" Her face hardened up even more.

I stood up. It was time to go. "Mom, we'll see where life takes me."

I lowered, kissed her on her forehead and left.

Discussion over.

I needed to think so I went home. I drove straight home.

I needed to think about what I was going to do, and how. Dad was talking with Detective Gracen today and we were supposed to meet either tonight or tomorrow to discuss the next steps. I'd be seeing Lana in a little while and I wanted to have some plan to talk about with her.

I needed to clear my mind to think. It was just hard knowing where to start.

I needed to think of motive. I considered if it was better to hire a P.I. to find Larissa. Or was that going in the wrong direction?

In the past there was only one thing that could clear my mind.

I went to the attic, grabbed my paint set, the easel and a canvas.

It was like they called to me.

I took them outside and just started to paint.

Seventeen years and I hadn't done this.

My hands remembered what to do.

But unlike my landscapes, I found myself doing something I'd never specialized in.

People weren't my style. I could paint a person but I'd always felt that I couldn't quite capture the emotion fully.

Not so now as my mind and my hands flew across the canvas creating from memory the image of Amelia.

It was her in the park she used to take Lana and me when we were kids.

I remembered looking at her and thinking she had the most beautiful smile.

She did.

Earlier Mom asked me if my path involved Lana.

It did. It still did.

It may seem like I was jumping ahead and maybe shooting myself in the foot. Especially with everything going on.

It might be the worst timing, but I knew what I wanted. I knew what I needed and I wanted to fight for it.

I wanted Lana back on my path. I made her fall for me once.

I'd do it again.

There was so much loss.

Too much loss. It was time to change things up.

Nothing could quite express the way I felt when I lost her the first time. *Powerless and helpless.*

I wasn't that anymore.

CHAPTER 19

Ryan

Seventeen years ago...

I'd made up my mind and I was going to do it.

It...

There were several 'its' in my plan.

The plan to leave this godforsaken college which I knew was classed as highly esteemed. Just not for me. The plan to go to New York with Lana, and...the other plan I had that topped all of that.

I glanced at Lana in my room. She was packing her

things for our trip to Charlotte. She got here last night and we had the most amazing time. Today we were going to the little hotel we'd christened our hideaway.

It overlooked the woods and felt like the place I wanted us to settle down in eventually.

God, had I changed and I'd be damned if I'd ever believe anyone who told me I'd be like this. I'd be this guy who was planning on asking his girl to marry him.

I'd completely changed around, even stopped smoking too. That was something I'd never planned to give up, but did it because while Lana thought it made me look cool, she worried about what it was doing to my health.

Anything for my girl, so I stopped.

"Ryan why do have so much chocolate?" She giggled, rushing over to grab a handful of chocolate eggs.

I smiled at her.

How was it possible that she looked more beautiful than just this morning.

"The guy down the hall is a chocoholic. He insisted I have these," I answered, moving over to her to pull her into my arms.

She slipped her arms around me and smiled at first, then gave me that worried look she'd given me since I'd told her my plans for New York.

"You have that face again princess." I pressed my forehead to hers.

"I'm worried Ryan. I just want you to be sure you're doing the right thing. Leaving college is a big thing. It just feels like I'm going to Parsons to get qualified in what I want to do and you're leaving here. It's Georgetown."

She lifted her head slightly so she could look at me.

"Lana, I don't want to be here. I came for the year like I promised myself I would and I hate it just as much as I did when it was just an idea. Law isn't me."

I was going to take the year out and see what I could do in the art world. Then I thought of applying to art school in New York. I had it all covered.

"Your family are gonna lose it when they find out. Your mom especially."

"Don't worry about her. Time to truly start living, princess." I smirked and gave her a wicked smile. "I want to talk to your mom about us."

"Really? Ryan I'm just scared and worried over how we'll pull this off."

"Princess, me talking to your mom is more important than anything. I hope she'll be happy for us. It would make things easier since I'm not going anywhere." I wasn't. Me telling her mother I was seeing her daughter was a matter of formality. Respect.

We'd been seeing each other for over two years. Sneaking around and seeing each other in secret.

Look at this beautiful girl in my arms.

Why the hell would I want to keep her secret?

No one would.

"I like that since you're kind of stuck with me"

"How stuck? Are we talking for the weekend or longer?" I teased.

She stood on the tips of her toes and kissed me. "I love you Ryan O'Shea. You're stuck with me for life. Where you go I follow."

"I love you Lana Connell. Where you go I follow too."

And that meant New York.

We were young and people might call us dumb and fools to love, but we knew what we were.

I knew what we were and it was true that where she went I followed.

That was how I wanted us to be for the rest of our lives.

Where was she...

There was no way she'd be late.

Something must have happened to her.

I imagined her crying somewhere grief-stricken for Amelia.

I imagined the worst.

It was natural given what had happened.

I'd never had anyone die on me before.

And... Amelia... I still couldn't accept it. Still couldn't believe it.

God...

It still didn't feel real to me. Amelia dead.

It didn't feel real to think it.

Two months ago Lana and I were in my room back at Georgetown. Life looked so promising then. We were going to leave for New York that same week. It was the end of semester and the start of the summer vacation break. Perfect.

Except it wasn't.

Lana got a call the following morning from Dad telling her what happened to Amelia. I still remember her screams of pain and loss.

Her mother killed herself. There were so many questions, so much of everything.

Now I couldn't find Lana. We were supposed to meet an hour ago and I couldn't find her.

We were going to New York tonight.

Our stuff had already gone ahead to the apartment I'd gotten for us and our flight was in a few hours so there was time. I just wished I knew where she was.

I'd looked everywhere for her. Everywhere I thought she could be.

Now I was wondering if I'd pushed this too much.

Two months of being back at my parents, crying

and going through the hell of being somewhere her mother should be but wasn't any more. I'd thought it was a good idea to go ahead with our plans.

Plus I felt that us having our privacy as a couple gave me more room to take care of her the way I wanted.

The funeral was what got to me the most and pushed me to do this.

Bad enough that her aunt didn't show, but I saw that look in her eyes of deep remorse. It was the look of someone who'd lost everything.

I wanted to take care of her and make sure she still got her dream.

I felt that was what Amelia would have wanted. She would have wanted to know that her girl got her dreams.

That was where I came in.

I'd tell my parents about us and me moving up there once we got settled in.

Right now I just needed to find Lana.

I went back to the last place I thought she'd be, which was the first place I'd looked.

Home.

I went straight there and my heart sank when she was nowhere to be found.

Jesus Christ, where was she?

I ended up in the library. Distressed, hopeless,

powerless.

Out of options.

I pulled out my phone and called her again. It was perhaps the two hundredth call I'd made. Just like before the phone rang out to her voicemail.

I didn't leave a message this time.

My heart ached, wanting an answer. Anything to give me an explanation of where she was.

What was she doing?

I just wanted to take care of her and help her get through this horrendous time. I hoped she knew that.

Maybe she'd lost her phone.

Maybe that was it.

That had to be why she wasn't answering. Lana always answered on the first ring.

When footsteps echoed behind me I whirled around hoping it was her.

It wasn't though. It was Mom.

"Mom, have you seen Lana?" I asked.

She came up to me and looked me over with concern. "Not in the last hour son. Is everything okay? Stupid question given what we've been through. You just look flustered."

"You saw her in the last hour?" I ignored the rest of her observation. I wasn't okay and I didn't have time to explain why. I just wanted to find Lana.

"Yes, she said something about seeing a friend in

Charlotte. I offered to give her a ride to the station but she wanted to be alone. I'm worried Ryan. She took a bag. It looked like she may stay overnight."

All I could do was stare at her.

What was she saying to me?

Lana went to Charlotte to see a friend and she left an hour ago with a bag?

What the fuck?

"Mom, are you sure she said Charlotte?"

We were supposed to be meeting at the coffeehouse in town. She'd wanted to get a few things and I had stuff of my own to do. We'd left each other this morning with the plan to meet at three. It was seven now. Our flight was at nine thirty.

"I'm positive. What's going on Ryan?" Her eyes searched mine. "Is she okay?" She brought a hand to her heart and winced.

"I don't know."

"Oh heavens. I'm going to contact your father. We have to find her. The poor girl. She mustn't be alone at this time. It's important that we're there for her as much as we can be. She needs to know we're here for her."

Numbness filled me as I nodded.

Charlotte... why would she go there?

This was my fault. I'd pressured her too much. I should have backed off.

"I'm going to see if I can catch up with her at the station." I'd go there first then head to Charlotte.

There could only be one place she'd go to. There was a little hotel we liked to stay at when we went there. She had to have been heading there.

Lana didn't tend to go anywhere else there, and she'd never been there without me.

I rushed away, my legs taking me as fast as possible. Then I drove away equally fast after I jumped in my car.

Lana where are you?

Princess, where are you?

CHAPTER 20

LANA

PRESENT DAY ...

I'd gathered more strength.

It came with the fire that burned within me for justice.

My body was still quite weak from the crying and the shock of the news but in my head I'd mustered up the courage to be brave.

That zeal for justice carried me to Detective Gracen's office.

I sat before him now, still fragile, but trying to focus.

He straightened up in his chair and continued to stare at me. It seemed like he was contemplating the best way to talk to me.

We'd practically sat in silence for the last few minutes. I appreciated his patience with me, and compassion.

"How are you feeling today?" he asked.

I shook my head. "I'm not sure." I met his concern-filled gaze with the pain in my eyes and his brows lowered.

"I am truly sorry Lana." He nodded. "When we first met I'd hoped it wouldn't come to this."

I pressed my hands into my thighs. It was a nervous habit I used to have. That and sweaty palms. So when I did both there would be two wet patches on my thighs that would always look odd.

I raised my shoulders and mirrored the way he sat, straightening up too.

"You knew... Didn't you?" I had to ask because looking back to that meeting we'd had a few weeks ago, I couldn't help but think he suspected this.

It was his body language and the things he'd said. What he'd said about me not getting to know him on a personal level. And that last thing about questioning. It all lended to some deeper level of suspicion and prep for something that might happen.

The prelude.

It was what you called a prelude. All of it. From the time I left Wilmington until now - that was a prelude and this was the main event.

Detective Gracen nodded slowly, confirming my thoughts.

"It's hard when you're dealing with nice people. Normal people who clearly loved their lost ones. I first started working this unit twenty years ago." He pressed his fists together and his eyes clouded. "A little girl went missing. We looked for her for a year. The parents were beside themselves with worry. They were a mess. A complete mess. Who was a mess too was the girl's uncle. Almost more than the parents."

He stopped for a moment like it was difficult to continue. "Lana, I confess that I go with my gut. I go with my gut and my heart next. It sounds like crazy talk to a lot of cops because how can you? Anyway, my gut told me something was off. This guy being more devastated than the parents showed deeper remorse. To me it did. A year of looking and I went on my own rogue mission following my gut instinct that told me this guy knew more than what we had on record. I followed him and noticed he kept going to a particular spot by the lake. He'd start crying. He'd go there, stand there for a few minutes and start crying." He rested his arms on the table and his shoulders tensed. "To the casual bystander he looked like the grieving uncle who might have been reminiscing about his days spent with his little niece by the lake. *But fuck*, to me I saw something else. Instinct make me call a team to the site and we found the bones of the girl's body. It turned out he'd killed her. He wanted his brother's wife and she refused him so he kidnapped the little girl to hold her as ransom. She tried to escape and he caught up with her and took out his frustration on her, hitting her with a rock. To this day he'll say he didn't know what came over him, or why he did it. The moral of the story is; things are not always what they seem. You have to push deeper to get to the crux of the matter. No matter the cost."

The tears that I'd been holding back spilled down my cheek and I pulled in a breath, loosening the constriction in my lungs. I didn't realize I hadn't been breathing the whole time he spoke.

What a heart-rending story. It tugged on my heart in so many ways.

I nodded, showing my understanding.

"My gut told me she never killed herself. My mom never killed herself. I was stuck between sticking to my guns about what I personally believed and what I saw or was told to believe. It didn't make sense."

"It never usually does at first. When the pieces of the puzzle start coming together it all fits and you wonder how you never saw it before, or how you missed something so obvious," he surmised. "Lana, I will tell you this too, that when I decided to reopen the investigation I probably didn't have as much evidence or support as you normally need to do that. I'm trusted here and if I say something looks off people jump to attention and look into it."

"How did you come by the case?" I was pretty certain he'd given a roundabout answer to that when we first met but what I was asking was a very different question.

He smiled a little smile that didn't exactly show humor. It was more for effect. As if he liked to show how right he could be. "I like snooping around. Comes with the title - Detective. From time to time I go over stuff. *Old cases.* I retire next year and maybe I just want to make sure I'm covering all bases before I go. So I was looking through some seriously old files in the archives. When I say old I mean old. Like from the last fifty years. I was the one who found the missing document from your mother's autopsy. It was just in the files randomly. Definitely didn't belong there. It looked like someone had misplaced it. Now this has come about I truly believe it got in the files by accident. I ran a search on it based on the reference number on the print out and that was when I found the details linking to your mother's case. Except the data on her files listed everything as inconclusive. Suspicion jumped out at me because I had a report that said otherwise. Couldn't read much into it because I'm not scientific but you get my drift."

"I do." I sighed.

"That was how this whole thing took off. Now Lana, it looks to me like someone went through a lot of trouble to A- kill your mother and make it look like a suicide and B- infiltrate the coroner's office and work things to their advantage from this side. Do you know anyone like that?"

I was waiting for that question. It was one I'd asked myself hundreds of times.

"No." I shook my head. That was the answer I'd come up with over and over again.

He held my gaze and inclined his head to the side. "When we met first, you said you saw your mother crying and she mentioned your aunt. Have you thought there might be a connection there?"

"I have. Detective Gracen, since I got this news I've been thinking of everything, and everyone. Everyone who could fit. I can't think of anybody. I can't." I brushed away a tear and dabbed at my eyes. "I feel like a failure right now, because I'm supposed to be able to help. I spent so much time with her. You'd think I'd know if a person evil enough to kill her existed."

"Don't blame yourself. Think back to my story

about the little girl. No one suspected the uncle. Why would they? His grief surpassed the girl's parents. In your case I suspect someone walking around wearing a mask. People do that. They cover up who they really are. If we'd simply found that she'd been murdered I would be looking out on a wider spectrum, but the document … the document and the way it was discovered, the way it was omitted and the way it was all set up to show something tells me more. I don't think we're looking at someone she didn't know, it was someone she knew."

I sucked in a sharp breath. "Someone she knew?"

He leaned forward and tapped the desk. "Let's leave it here, girl. I will do the rest. That was just to prepare you and maybe jog your memory."

I looked at him, noted the firmness in his eyes and realized just like I did at that first meeting that he suspected more than he was saying.

He looked like he had a suspect in mind.

God in heaven… he actually had a suspect in mind.

"Who do you think it is?" I asked outrightly.

He shook his head at me. "Let's leave it here Lana. I've probably said more than I should."

I bit the inside of my lip and nodded, accepting. Knowing I'd have to wait to find out.

I headed back to Ryan's house.

We'd planned to meet up there.

While I'd gone to see Detective Gracen, Ryan went to meet with a private investigator in town.

I couldn't wait to see him to find out if there was anything he'd thought about.

What would he think though, when I told him all the ideas that Detective Gracen believed.

Detective Gracen had a suspect in mind and wouldn't say who it was. That could mean so many things.

It could be that he didn't want to say anything because there wasn't enough evidence as yet to incriminate the person. It could also mean there was and he was holding off telling me because of procedure.

Also, I got the impression that he was a compassionate person. Maybe he didn't want to tell me just yet because it would hurt me.

So the grand question was; who did he think it was?

Fuck...

I hated all of this.

Everything.

I never imagined any of this happening and feeling so damn powerless was killing me slowly, like poison working its way through my body and there was nothing I could do to stop it.

I didn't know what the hell I would have done if I'd been alone in this.

Knowing I had others around me offering their help and support alleviated the burden in a big way.

Helpless and useless as I'd felt, it gave me something to hope for.

Ryan and his father were doing their best.

Georgie was also arranging her flight. She'd sounded sick on the phone and as much as I'd begged her not to come she insisted on being with me as soon as she could.

Much as I wanted her to stay in LA, I knew in my heart that having her here with me would help massively.

It helped to give me the strength I lacked. It was something I never had before. I was just tossed into the deepest end of the ocean and had to swim.

Sometimes it still felt like I was still swimming around trying to make my way back, trying to make my way back to a life I'd wanted so badly. It was just that life had changed drastically. The person who I'd wanted so badly to be at the shoreline waiting for me to surface wouldn't be there.

Mama wouldn't be there ever again because someone killed her, someone took her away from me.

The thought made me tear up again but blinked back the tears so I could focus.

When I turned the corner to Ryan's house, I saw a red Mercedes parked on the drive. I didn't know who that was and I wasn't really prepared to see anyone else by myself. Ryan's car wasn't there so this person was in his house alone.

What if it was his mother?

Jesus Lord, if it was her... with the way I felt I wouldn't hesitate to rain Armageddon upon her. I mean end of the bible, Book of Revelations style Armageddon. God himself would have to come down from heaven and calm me down.

That was the mood I was in. I'd felt compassion myself and figured she was sick so of course she wouldn't have been around with everyone else.

But I wasn't stupid. While I'd figured that, I was sure by now she knew I was back in town and it wasn't like I could forget the reason I'd left.

She would stay away from me because it was wise. There was no way she'd want her precious family to know what she was really like.

I parked my car and got out.

Pausing for a moment at the bottom of the steps leading up to the house, I caught one last breath of fresh air to clear my head.

A breath and a silent prayer that the person inside wasn't Ryan's mom.

On that breath I proceeded up the steps and opened the door. Ryan had given me a key for the house.

I went inside and footsteps echoed against the wooden steps of the stairs.

When a naked blonde woman flashing a satin dressing gown in her hands came into view, my mouth dropped. On seeing me, she shrieked and covered herself.

My mouth sunk further into the fucking ground when I recognized her.

Tiffany!

Tiffany Tate.

"What the hell are you doing here?" Those were the first words to fly from my mouth.

This bitch had put me through so much when I was growing up. I was helpless then. Not so now, not so at all.

She had the audacity to snarl at me and look at me as if I was the one who was out of place in this scene. She looked exactly the way she did when I'd found her in my room that time, back at the O'Shea mansion. Although it was clear she'd had work done on her face, she didn't look all that much different.

"*Me?* You're asking me that? Are you kidding me? What are you doing here?"

"I asked first." I stood my ground. "What are *you* doing in Ryan's house."

"I'm his wife. I think I have whatever right I want to be here."

Shock flew straight through me. It washed over me starting from my eyes as I eyed her with astonishment. Then it cascaded from there to my toes.

Ryan's wife…

He'd married Tiffany?

My Ryan got married to her, the one person I hated the most.

She was who he was talking about.

He was divorced but she was here calling herself his wife and she'd come down the stairs naked like it was normal for her to do that.

Back in high school they were always on and off. Maybe this was the same fucking thing.

Jesus Christ, why was everything so fucked up.

The door flung open behind me and Ryan came in looking flustered.

He looked from me to Tiffany, scanned over what she was barely wearing and shook his head.

"Fuck no." He growled, nostrils flared. "Fucking hell no." It was then that he looked back to me.

"You married her?" I scuffed. God, in the grand scheme of things this was so far down the rung.

I had no right to ask him that. I had no right to want to know anything of his private life. It was just that it was *her*.

"Lana please, you know we're divorced," he answered.

"So the answer is yes." I rushed past him heading back to my car.

I really didn't want to feel like the sixteen year old again who'd just seen the boy she liked making out with the girl who everyone thought was the most beautiful in the school. I didn't want to feel like that today, or ever.

Ryan rushed up to me and caught me. Not just grabbing my arm but actually caught me, slipping his arm around my waist and picking me up, stopping me in flight and pulling me flush against his chest.

"Please, don't go," he begged. *"Please."* It was the agony in his voice that must have reached the place in my heart that loved him.

He held me for a few seconds and set me down.

I turned to face him and shook my head. "Ryan, you got married to Tiffany Tate?"

"Lana, all kinds of shit happened to me six years ago. I literally fell down the rabbit hole when you left. Then I saw you in LA and I let you go. I came back a mess and she seduced me when I was drunk out of my damn mind. The next time I saw her she told me she was pregnant." He stopped and my heart stretched with the revelation of more news. A child. "It was some elaborate trick because the baby wasn't mine. I found out last year that my son isn't mine and it crushed me. I'm really sorry I didn't tell you before. I'm truly sorry. It's just more shit to add to everything else, more that happened to me that I wished hadn't."

Shit!

This was all my fault.

All from one thing leading to another.

I'd left him believing his life would be better, but it wasn't. Everything, he'd told me was all horrible. There wasn't one thing I could hold on to that happened to him that was good.

Nothing at all.

This was what happened to him.

He got married to Tiffany …

It was too much. All of it.

I couldn't deal with it. "I'm sorry..."

He reached for me but I backed away and the hurt in his eyes gripped me.

"Lana..."

"I'm sorry I left you. I really am."

"Don't go. Don't leave again." His eyes pleaded with me.

I drew in a ragged breath feeling lightheaded. "I need some space. There's too much. Too much going on Ryan. I just..."

I couldn't continue. Nothing I said felt like it was the right thing.

BELLA FONTAINE & KHARDINE GRAY

I really did need some space and strength.

Only one person could give me that.

I left him standing there, jumped in my car and fled, heading to the cemetery to see Mama.

I'd only been once and that was for the funeral.

After I'd left I tried to come back to visit her grave. I couldn't do it. I even went as far as hiring someone to tend to the plot on a weekly basis, doing a job I should have been doing for the last seventeen years. I couldn't do it though because it meant accepting she wasn't with me anymore.

Today was the day of acceptance because I needed her and that was the only place I knew I'd find her.

CHAPTER 21

RYAN

THANK FUCK when I went back inside the house Tiffany was dressed in actual clothes.

She knew not to fuck with me when I breezed back inside the house ready to combust with fury.

If she was a guy... *I would...*

I balled my fists at my side and shook the thought free from my mind.

I didn't even like thinking like that because it meant acknowledging I was totally tempted to hit her, and I was. I hated any kind of violence against women. Thought, or otherwise.

"What are you doing here?" I asked in a cold steady voice.

She stepped forward from where she was and brought her hands together.

"I came to see you."

"Looked like you came to more than see me." She was naked under that dressing gown when I came in.

God knew what Lana must have seen and thought. How did Tiffany even get inside the house?

Fuck. It didn't matter.

There was so much shit on my mind and I needed to weed out the trash like what was happening now to free it up to deal with the real problems.

The real problems that just got another added to it.

Lana drove off and left, upset, and I felt the connection we'd built up over the last few weeks snap.

Tiffany looked down at the wooden floor and her gaze climbed up to meet mine.

"Your mother told me you still loved me very much and that I should try to break the ice. I came here to do that," she explained.

I narrowed my eyes and my brows snapped together. "When the fuck did she tell you that?"

"Yesterday, after we saw each other. She told me you said you wanted to give me another chance but you were too afraid to try, but the love was always there."

Holy fuck!

What the hell was Mom playing at?

I couldn't have expressed more opposite words.

"No," I breathed and she brought her hands up to her cheeks.

"No? It's not true?"

"Tiffany. None of that is true. You know the extent of my feelings for you from what I've specifically said and that's disgust. It's disgust."

I wouldn't have normally been so crass and crude, or abrasive. Those however were my true feelings spilling out. I'd had enough of everything.

I was done with the shit and pussyfooting around. Why would Mom do this to me?

Force Tiffany on me when she must have gotten from my conversation with her that I wanted to be with Lana.

"Ryan I have apologized so many times. I have been in love with you my whole life. I made a mistake and I went the wrong way about everything. None of that meant I didn't love you."

"Are you kidding me? You tried to pass another man's child off as mine. *Jack.* Tiffany I love that child so much and blood might mean nothing to me but one day it might to him. He feels like mine but he will never be. You lied and you schemed and you're here telling me this bullshit."

"It's because of her isn't it?" she spat, ignoring all of

what I'd said. "Her, she was always in the way. All you did was use me to make her jealous."

That part was true. Not my finest moment but true. It wasn't however like she suffered in the mix from it.

"That is irrelevant to the shambles of a marriage we had. Don't act like you're the fucking victim here." I threw back.

"Irrelevant? We'll see how irrelevant the past is when I stop you from seeing Jack!"

I wasn't sure what spark of an idea flickered off in that head of hers to make her say that to me.

Threaten me?

Really?

Seemed like she'd forgotten who I was.

I picked up the vase Mom got me for Christmas and threw it across the room. It crashed into the wall and sent shards of glass everywhere as it shattered.

She shrieked, scared and rushed to the corner as I moved for her.

She thought I was going to grab her, what she didn't know was I could have won an award for my self control.

"Tiffany." I chuckled, dark with the fury that now roiled within me. "Don't you fucking dare threaten me! Don't fuck with me and don't threaten me. *Ever.* I know the law. I know I have no rights to Jack, or else we wouldn't be having this conversation."

The only people who could give me the permission I sought to have my little boy in my life were his biological parents. Since we didn't know who his father was that meant the ball was in her court.

"I'm no one's fool and I won't be yours. You won't play me like you did before." I added. "You tricked me once before and you won't do it again with threats. I pay for everything you have. The house, the car outside, the fucking shit you keep injecting your face with. If you mess with me I'll make sure Jack gets taken away from you."

"You can't do that," she whimpered.

The smile came back to my face. "You fucking evil bitch. *Try me.* Look... at *my* face *Tiffany*. I'm serious as fuck. This is the last time we'll have a conversation like this. If you cross me you won't like it. You will lose everything and I will make sure I'm the only parent who'll have access to Jack. Blood or not. *Understood?*"

I had to admit there was a sensation of relief, of a burden lifted as she nodded. She nodded agreement and her shoulders fell.

"Good. Now here's what you're going to do." I raised my finger like I was making a point. "Set up visitation rights, allow me to see my child and that is all. I will continue to send you whatever you need. I will continue to pay for everything. You just leave me alone."

Tears welled in her eyes as she nodded.

I stepped away from her, allowing her passage to leave.

She moved away but stopped, turned and looked back to me. "I still love you Ryan."

I looked away. Away from her and over to the long French windows.

Whatever she felt for me didn't matter anymore. It never did.

She left and the door closed.

I sighed, frustrated and looked around the place. Broken glass everywhere and the tension still in the air.

Mom...

I couldn't let this go. It was too important and actually below the belt.

She basically told Tiffany to seduce me.

This was the last thing I wanted to deal with now. I'd made progress this morning with the P.I.

I had a lead on some drug dealers who were looking for Larissa years ago. She'd skipped town just after Amelia died and no one knew where she went.

She was still at large but the thing the P.I. found out was that she owed a mobster drug dealer called Frankie twenty grand. He'd threatened to kill her and her family if she didn't pay up.

I'd told the PI to pursue the lead. A mobster drug

dealer did sound like the sort of person who could have killed Amelia.

That was what I was going to tell Lana.

It would have to wait now.

That fury still blazed in me. It sent me straight to the mansion to see Mom and only subsided when I saw police cars on the drive.

Mom was outside bawling her eyes out while Dad was being led away by an officer.

He was in handcuffs.

I didn't know the nightmare could get any worse than it already was.

It could.

It fucking did.

The police had Dad in custody on suspicion of murdering Amelia on account of them questioning an anonymous witness who placed him with Amelia at the DoubleTree. It was conclusive to the time period that she died. It looked like Dad would have been the last person to see her alive.

I was offering legal representation.

The officers must have had him for three hours booking him in. I waited outside in the visitors lounge for them to finish.

BELLA FONTAINE & KHARDINE GRAY

Mom was at home, probably beside herself with worry but I couldn't think about her now.

Dad couldn't have killed Amelia.

I knew he would never do something like that. He would never kill anyone.

However, someone being able to place him at the DoubleTree around the timeframe in which Amelia was murdered raised enough suspicion to work with. Records from the DoubleTree released an hour ago, listing him as staying the night there with her cemented it.

When the officers were finished with him I was able to see him.

We met in his jail cell. He looked like the shell he'd spoken of weeks ago when he described me.

His skin was so pale and his eyes were void of the man I knew.

I sat in front of him and looked him over.

He kept his eyes on the hard gray concrete of the jail cell, not looking at me. Shame was all over his face.

I moved and sat next to him, placing an arm around his shoulders. The gesture was the only thing that seemed to create some response from him.

He twisted his head around to face me and released a short sigh.

"Tell me what happened Dad." I nodded. "Tell me.

This is off the record. It's just you and me. Tell me what happened."

More shame filled his eyes and I had a feeling I knew what he was going to

tell me.

Could almost guess it.

"I had an affair with Amelia," he confessed.

I couldn't feign surprise because I think deep down I always knew. Hearing it

though was hard. I would never have pegged dad as the kind of man who would do that.

"I never killed her Ryan. I couldn't... I loved her," he added, and he reminded me of the person I'd witnessed that night I spied on him with Amelia in the library. I could tell something was going on. The signs were there.

"I know," I replied and his gaze sharpened. "I know you didn't kill her, but I also know that you loved her, more than Mom."

He hung his head down. "I didn't want any of this to happen ... I didn't mean for any of it to. It just did. Ryan, I asked your mother repeatedly for a divorce but she wouldn't give me one. I doubt she knew about me and Amelia. It doesn't make it right. I may be this badass lawyer in the courtroom but every time your mother begged me to give her a chance I did. I shouldn't have because it wasn't fair. I didn't love her, and love isn't something you force. She changed a lot after we got married. She changed and became this person I didn't recognize. The wealth went to her head and she started treating people who didn't have what we had like they were nothing. It was the first sign of ugliness and I drifted away. Then Amelia came on the scene and I think I fell for her straight away."

I loosened my hold on him. "How long did it last?'

More shame filled his eyes. "On and off for five years. She didn't want to continue the secret. Neither did I. Days before I took her to the DoubleTree she broke it off, then I came to her and showed her a fresh set of divorce papers I planned to issue your mother. That was the only thing that made her go with me. Seeing the evidence that I was serious about us."

As he spoke, something sharp tugged on my heart.

I understood what he was saying. I did, but all of it just landed him in the prime suspect seat for being with her.

"Dad... this doesn't look good."

"I know kid. I know."

I sat with him for a while, the two of us in silence until the guard came to get me. I promised to come back first thing.

As I was leaving I spotted a familiar head of dark velvet hair swooped to the side as the young woman it belonged to leaned against the wall in the foyer.

Lana.

It was Lana. She lifted her head when she saw me and rushed into my arms.

I held her, grateful for her presence. Grateful she was here and with me.

"He didn't do it Ryan," she gushed, pulling back so she could look at me. "I know he didn't. The same way I always knew in my heart that my mother didn't kill herself I know your father didn't kill her."

"Thank you… He would never have hurt her."

"I know. I know."

Another burden eased off my shoulders, hearing her say that.

I knew dad was innocent.

It meant so much more to hear her say it too.

But what did we do now?

Where did I go from here?

CHAPTER 22

LANA

WE ENTERED Ryan's house and he turned on the lights.

It felt strange being back here when just hours ago I'd left in such a massive state of confusion.

Feeling overwhelmed, I'd gone to the cemetery, found Mama's grave and cried until my soul stopped weeping.

I'd felt guilty for not being back, because I actually did feel close to her. If such a thing were possible I felt the warmth of her. The glow that always came from her was there.

When I left I went back to my place to think.

That was when I got the phone call.

Detective Gracen called me. When he told me Mr. O'Shea had been arrested and there was enough evidence to bring him in for suspicion of murdering Mama I didn't believe it.

And it wasn't because I was a fool trying to hold on to a façade. I knew it in my heart.

It was the way he always looked at her, with so much love in his eyes.

Then I got confirmation of it when Ryan filled me in on the missing pieces.

Could I be surprised when he'd told me his father had an affair with my mother?

No, not so much.

It was that way Mr. O'Shea always looked at her. I'd seen him many times and then there was the way he was willing to do anything for her, and for me.

As a child I saw him as this kind person who wanted to make us happy, and he was. He still was. But it was still a mess.

What a tangle of mess.

What a damn tangle of knots tighter than macramé.

Secrets, lies, more secrets and more lies.

Skeletons were falling out of the closet whispering secrets from their lips.

I felt soon the whispers would become deafening. Soon the whispers would become screams.

It reminded me of my own secret.

As I was at Mama's grave, all the words of inspiration everyone had filled me with over the weeks came to me. The conclusion I came to was: Think of what you want most.

Ryan walked over to the fireplace and rested his hand on the river rocks that decorated the outside of the mantel piece.

I gazed at him and knew I had the answer.

What I wanted most was him.

Same answer as always.

With everything happening I just wanted to leave it all outside like it never happened, and just be us. The way we used to be.

I walked over to him and for the first time noticed the broken glass on the floor.

He saw me looking and shook his head. "I was frustrated."

"It's okay."

I slipped my arms around him and rested my head on his chest, listening to the steady rhythm of his heart.

"Lana, I'm sorry about the horrible day we've had. It has been too much for you. Maybe you should have your space. Time away from me."

I lifted my head and stared at the glorious blue of

his eyes. Shaking my head I stood on my toes and kissed him.

"I think seventeen years was enough space. It was such a long time and I was so lost without you." I bit the edge of my lip to stop myself from crying again. No more tears tonight.

"Me too." He nodded and I saw it all over his face. I could just imagine what it must have been like for him to be with Tiffany and find out their son wasn't his.

The thing was, it was just the sort of thing Tiffany would do, exactly the sort of thing.

"We have each other," I promised.

"Do we Lana? My father is in jail on suspicion of murdering your mother. How the hell do I get around that? So many secrets, even us."

I grimaced to think about it again. Of what his mother did to me.

I exhaled the thought and kissed him, giving him a kiss that spoke of how I felt. When he cupped my face the kiss turned greedy, then needy.

I needed him. Wanted him.

Had to have him.

In one swoop he picked me up and carried me up the stairs to the bedroom.

He set me down on the bed and we wrestled with the tangle of clothes until we were both naked. All the while he kissed me, all over, caressing my skin with the sweetness of his lips and the tenderness of his love.

I remember the first time we had sex, and I remembered the first time we made love. Two different things with different emotions, both representative of us.

Of who we were, what we were and what we wanted to be.

Right now was a combo of both.

As he stripped off his clothes too, parted my thighs and slid into me to start the wild sexual rhythm we both needed, the rawness of sex took over.

But... as he smoothed his hand over mine and pressed his forehead against mine while we moved, the purity of love flowed through us like a living force of energy.

Transcendental energy that lulled to the highest state of bliss and ecstasy.

That was what it felt like.

That was what we were. Always.

Always and again he gave me the answer to what I wanted most.

Had to be a reason why I kept getting the same answer. Had to be a reason why it had never changed.

So I should stop asking the question and accept the answer.

I had to be with him.

Even if I owned the whole fashion world empire

and I were the only person on earth designing clothes it wouldn't make me happy. I was a fool to think I was living before.

I valued my accomplishments and valued the journey I'd made to get as far as I had. However, there was no substitute for what I experienced with the man I'd lost seventeen years ago.

Later that night I lay in his arms.

Neither of us spoke and I knew what he was thinking. He was worried about his father. I was too. I truly was, mainly because of Detective Gracen. If he was sure what hope did we have with our own beliefs?

So many things coursed through my mind. There was one thing I should do though, or at least the prelude to it.

I ran my fingers over Ryan's chest. He responded by catching my hand and bringing it to his lips to kiss my knuckles.

I straightened up and looked at him.

"Where you go I will follow," I breathed and he straightened up.

"What?"

"Where you go, I will follow," I repeated with a little smile. It was a thing we used to say to each other.

Our relationship went through different stages. There was the first part where he'd been this badass guy I shouldn't have liked, who put me through hell when he was teasing me and when he wasn't. I called that the kissing phase. It was the part where I wasn't sure if he was just playing with my emotions. Then he told me he was mine and it all changed. We became the couple.

The guy and the girl who were always together and couldn't get enough of each other.

Wherever he went I followed. Wherever I went he followed me too.

I gave him another smile.

"Lana I dare not think of what that means. I know what I want you to mean."

"It means what it always meant Ryan. It never changed. When you came to my office in LA and I saw you, I couldn't believe I'd lived so long without you in my life. Coming back home here to the past has told me that I can't be without you. I don't want to." That was a truth I'd been trying to escape for years.

He leaned forward and kissed me.

"I love you," he whispered against my lips.

I didn't think that being told those words by the same man seventeen years later would have even more of an effect than when I heard them the first time.

I never knew.

I never knew.

I also never knew that the love I felt for him could have surpassed what I already felt.

"I love you too. I love you Ryan. I love you. I never stopped. Not once. Not even a little bit. Never." My throat closed up when I cast my mind back to when I'd left.

He cupped my face when he saw my anguish. "Princess... please, please tell me what happened... Why'd you leave? Why? It doesn't fit. You would have contacted me or something. You wouldn't have just left me."

"I don't want to hurt you even more. There's been enough pain today with your father. Enough secrets." Now wasn't the time to add his mother to the mix.

He shook his head though. "This isn't about me. It's been about you all along. My girl disappeared seventeen years ago and I didn't know what happened to her. There's not much left in this world to hurt me, other than keeping the truth no matter what it is, Lana. All of this has been about damn secrets and lies. No more, so please... tell me."

"I don't know where to start." I closed my eyes and my stomach knotted.

The slight caress of his finger on my cheek made me open my eyes to gaze at him.

He dropped his hand to his lap and shuffled to face me.

"Start from the beginning...We'd sat in bed just like this... at my parents' house. It was morning. You'd been crying and because you weren't eating I said I'd go get you a bagel. I got it for you and I started talking about New York to distract you. Do you remember?" He nodded, looking at me with wide expectant eyes.

"I remember. You got me the bagel and I started to nibble on it and I said Mama liked bagels. Then I started to cry again."

"Then I said, she wanted me to make sure you ate. She'd want me to take care of you so I helped you eat it. You wanted to get some stuff in town to travel with. I thought you needed some time to be alone so I allowed you to go."

"I said I'll see you at three and..." This was it...

The moment of truth. More than a reckoning.

"And what, princess?"

"I got back to the house to grab the last of my things. Your mother was waiting for me in my room."

The minute I said that he tensed and narrowed his eyes at me.

"My... *mother?*"

"Your mother. She said she heard us talking and knew we'd been together. She knew we were planning to leave for New York and you weren't going back to college." I stopped.

He was looking at me with such great intensity that

it made me more anxious. Made me more nervous to tell him.

Now that I'd started talking, started the process of revealing what happened, I couldn't exactly stop. I had to look away from him as I continued.

"She was packing up all my stuff in a bag. Wasn't much because a lot of my important stuff was already in New York. I asked her what she was doing and she asked me if I thought the maid's daughter was good enough for her son, and didn't I think you deserved someone better than me. She said… you'd worked hard to get to where you were and you deserved a life in a profession you wanted. Something you could hold high as an achievement…" I stopped to take a breath, but continued to look away from him. This was difficult. "She didn't think a tramp like me would understand. After all, my mother and I were like trash and she did us a favor when she gave my mother a job. She told me to get out of her house. Take my things and leave, take my things and leave and never come back. Never look back. And if I tried to contact you or anyone she'd destroy me. She'd do everything in her power to destroy me."

I'd said enough for him to understand what happened. It was a good summary with the main points that elicited the reaction I'd expected from him.

He stood up, almost bolting up out of the bed.

It was the abrupt action that made me look up at him.

Ryan was actually shaking.

The shock on his face turned his skin pale and his eyes wide with terror.

"What are you telling me Lana?" His voice quivered.

I stared at him head on and hugged my knees to my chest.

"You know, at first I felt like a coward when I grabbed that bag and left." I hugged my knees tighter.

"I wished you'd come to me."

I shook my head. "No... Ryan. I wouldn't have. It wasn't the threat to destroy me that made me leave. It was the fact that I thought I wasn't good enough for you. I was already worried that you were throwing your life away for me, and that confirmed it."

"That wasn't true."

I raised my shoulders into a shrug. "Ryan, at the time I was too weak to fight or believe anything else. I'd just lost my mom and I was about to lose you too. Everything. I thought if I left you'd be who you were supposed to be. I thought that you'd become a successful lawyer and do everything you actually did. And I was right, you did it. You became that guy she wanted you to be. I knew that you loved me and when it came to me you'd always put me first, even when it could cost you. So I left." The tears slowly found their way down my cheeks.

He came over to me, dropped to his knees like he did the other day and took my hands.

"God… Lana… I'm so sorry." The sadness in his eyes gripped me. "I would never have guessed it was her. Nothing was further from the truth. It was me who wasn't good enough for you. You know what I'm like. I'm gifted to be good at a lot of stuff so it was a given that what I'm doing now would be successful. That had nothing to do with you going or staying."

"I just wanted to do what was right. I didn't want to stand in the way of your success."

"All I wanted was you. All I needed was you. That was all." He nodded with conviction, then a hardness I'd never seen before filled his eyes. "All that time we looked for you *she* … My mother told me you went to Charlotte. She said you went to see a friend. So that was the first place I went after searching for you all day."

"That's what she told you?" The hardness filled me too.

"That is what she told me. All the while she knew what she'd done. She acted like she was helping Dad and me search for you, saying how she couldn't believe you would just leave and not say anything. She didn't know why."

I held my tongue because now wasn't the time for me to talk.

"My... mother lied?" His eyes searched mine and I almost felt guilty for the nod of confirmation I gave him.

CHAPTER 23

RYAN

WE PARKED on the driveway at the mansion and just sat in the car.

Ten minutes had passed and we were both still here sitting side by side.

Tension thickened the atmosphere between us and around us.

It would be Lana's first time back here in seventeen years. First time back since Mom threw her out.

I was still trying to wrap my head around that as well as other things.

I was here to see her, and Lana was with me.

There was so much to work out here and I wasn't sure what to pick at first.

What Mom did to Lana, what Tiffany said about Mom, or…what Dad said about the affair.

The common denominator in everything was Mom.

Dad said he didn't think Mom knew about him and Amelia, but I knew different. After all wasn't I the one who saw her watching them that night in the library all those years ago.

She was watching them.

She knew what was happening, what was going on.

It was clear she knew. Thinking back now I could tell she knew from the manner in which she'd moved that night. That was why she was watching.

I'd sat here in the car stewing in anger. What Lana had told me about Mom was enough for me to cut my mother off. But… there was a feeling in my heart that whispered disaster.

It told me it was waiting.

Power was the key here.

It was the key in this whole scenario. Power to be able to do anything and have the resources to do it. My parents had it.

My mother had it.

I unhooked my seat belt. It was time. Time to talk to Mom.

I looked over at Lana who'd glanced at me as I undid the belt.

"I'm ready," I told her. "Ready to see her."

She nodded and I noticed the stern expression on her face.

We went inside and found Mom sitting by the fireplace.

Her face turned paler when her eyes landed on Lana.

"Oh, this is a pleasant surprise," she stated.

I remained expressionless, able to see through the shit of her phony act. I was actually offended that she'd tried it with me. As if I wasn't used to her dishing that shit out to other people.

"Look." I pointed at Lana. "I found her." It was as though the last seventeen years hadn't happened and I was continuing the same conversation from that day Lana left.

She knew what I meant from what I said and the way I said it.

"What's going on?" she asked.

I felt like a real asshole standing my ground because of how sick I knew she'd been. Right now it meant nothing.

"Lana told me what happened. She told me why she left. She told me what you did."

Mom stood up, showing a strength I didn't think she had and she faced Lana.

"And what did you tell my son?" she challenged Lana in that authoritative voice she'd used many times with the staff here.

"I don't need to tell you. You know. The time for me talking to you is past. It's him you need to speak to. Not me," Lana answered, unveiling the strong woman I'd seen when I found her in L.A.

Mom turned back to face me. The muscle quivered at her jaw and her mouth thinned with displeasure. "Such insolence, you would believe Lana over me? She's just like her whoring mother."

My whole body stiffened as though she'd struck me.

Her personality had just switched out on me. No way could this be the same woman who called Amelia family the other day. I couldn't believe what she just said.

"My mother wasn't a whore!" Lana lashed out.

Mom gave her a menacing smile enhanced by her skeletal features. "Oh look, she thinks she can talk big now that she has a piece of the pie and clearly my son. You'll never want for anything again will you? To me you'll always be scum."

"That is enough!" I roared. When she returned her focus to me and I looked in her eyes I saw the truth staring at me.

God... the little boy who used to look up to his mother wanted to hang on to the past and the pure vision of her.

But, I had to let him down.

I might not have wanted to be a lawyer but I became a damn good one. The pieces of the puzzle were all starting to come together. I wasn't sure if Lana saw it too.

My heart tried to hold me back from going further. I, however, always and ever the rebel, pushed back.

I was too consumed with everything to piece it all together last night.

Dad told me about the affair and that gave me an avenue. *A motive.*

It was a reason to want Amelia dead.

Someone with influence and power could do a lot.

"You knew about the affair didn't you? Dad and Amelia?" I aired.

Lana looked over at me when I said that.

"It went on for years," Mom answered, her voice steady. "Years. Can you believe it? My husband and my maid. Even before they started sleeping together. It was all in the eyes. The looks, the comments. A touch here and there."

"And what did you do about it, *Mom?*" From the corner of my eye I saw Lana's lips part.

"It started out with your father listening to Amelia

reading Lana poetry at bed time. Something so innocent yet deadly. I pretended not to know then one day I
saw them kissing in the secret garden by the river." She
turned to Lana. "Your mother was a whore dear. She
thought it was okay to steal people's husbands. She
stole mine. She was going to take mine away from me. I
found the divorce papers. Can you imagine how I felt? I
gave my life to a man who fell in love with my maid. I
had to put a stop to it and get rid of her."

Lana sucked in a breath.. "Get rid of her? It was
you?"

No matter what bravado Lana had assumed coming
in here, no matter what strength she gathered, it all left
her and all I could do was stare, beyond mortification.
Horrified at what I was hearing.

"Yesssssss." Mom sang in delight. "It was me."

Shock siphoned the blood from my body at the
declaration. Then the shock suffused my soul as she
continued in her chant of glee.

"A bottle to the head can do a lot. It can knock a
woman down and give you the chance to strangle her,"
Mom chanted. "All those books in the library and
friends in the right places can give a woman so many
ideas. It was all so clever. My friend with a truck, her
friend at the coroner's office. Then my stupid friend
who was supposed to make the paperwork go away. He

didn't do a very good job. Would have stopped people like Detective Gracen from snooping around. I just wanted my family back. My husband to be mine, and my son to have a chance to be with someone better, more of his league. I killed your mother. I killed that fucking bitch and watched the life drain from her body."

When Lana dropped to the ground in a flood of tears I rushed to her side. I went to her feeling like I had no right to touch her or be near her.

I felt vile.

My mother killed hers.

When I thought of Dad being a suspect it was bad enough.

Terrible.

This was beyond anything I could describe.

The little grip around my finger from Lana sparked the love I felt for her and I held her.

This was the disaster I could feel in my heart. It was what I'd sensed. I just wanted to be wrong.

I looked at Mom, at the wicked smile on her face and I actually felt bile rise in my throat. She took pleasure in all of this.

"I'm turning you in to the police," I told her. 'You will pay for what you did."

She shrugged in a nonchalant manner. "Go ahead." My threat didn't even faze her. "I have less than six months left to live. I no longer care."

I was pretty certain I should have felt like the world ended as she said that. I

was supposed to feel devastated and drained. She was my mother. The woman I loved with my soul. The person who stood before me however wasn't the one I believed her to be. The woman in front of us was a monster. A monster who was capable of dealing devastation, doom, death.

She'd killed Amelia.

I closed my eyes, squeezing them shut as my heart splintered into pieces. Broken in a way that I knew would never truly be fixed even if I tried.

CHAPTER 24

LANA

"How are you doing?" Detective Gracen asked. He straightened up in his habitual manner even though he wasn't at his desk.

He'd come by the house to see me.

"I don't know." I gave him a kind smile. It felt like the beginning of a wound that was starting to heal.

"It's like deja vu. Pretty sure you said that the other day." He smirked and reached for the little cup of tea Georgie had made for him and a cookie from Pat's deluxe range.

One good thing about having a best friend who had an amazing husband was that he took care of you too.

Pat had impressed me. He'd flown over with Georgie and insisted on doing absolutely everything for the both of us.

"These are good," Detective Gracen commented.

This was him it seemed when he was okay. When the case was closed.

"I'll let Pat know you like 'em." The power couple were in the kitchen cooking me dinner before they headed back to LA. They'd been here for the last three days.

All that time and I didn't see Ryan. He'd messaged and I knew there was a lot going on but I wanted to see him.

Detective Gracen pressed his lips together and the seriousness returned to his face.

"You've been through a lot, Lana. I hope you give yourself a break. I came to check on you. This was a rather difficult case," he confessed.

I nodded, wholeheartedly agreeing. "Words can't express."

Kathy had been taken into custody. There was talk about her going to a medium psychiatric secure unit to live out the rest of her life when she got sentenced.

I'd signed off at that point.

Like she said, she no longer cared. Neither did I.

I got the truth. it was a truth I never saw coming, or did I?

Detective Gracen looked me over with curiosity. "Do you feel it yet?"

"That feeling like there was something staring you right in the face this whole time and you can't believe you didn't see it?" I asked. "*Yes.*"

He nodded. "Yeah. When I asked you if there was anyone you thought it might be and I told you it would be someone your mother knew, I'd already narrowed my lists of suspects down to two people. I didn't have any evidence on Mrs. O'Shea, but exactly what happened is exactly what I'd suspected. Wife suspects her husband is cheating, finds out he is with the maid, wife kills the maid and makes it look like a suicide, wife takes one step further to cover her tracks by contacting a friend in the coroner's office to take care of things from our side."

A day after Mrs. O'Shea was taken in it was found that there were two people who helped her at the time. They were still looking for the person with the truck and whoever else might be involved.

"You knew I knew something deep down?"

"I hoped. It's all guesswork in the end. You watch the Mentalist?" He smiled.

I grinned. "I've seen a few episodes."

"It's great isn't it? I'm kind of like him. Push instinct

to the limit and fill in the blanks after. I only hoped you'd remember something when I'd told you it would be someone your mother knew. Only a powerful person with money could pull off what happened. There could only have been a few people in your lives like that. Anyway... case closed. The truth is out and it's painful. It always is no matter how it reveals itself. The focus now is what next?"

"Yeah."

"Going back to LA?" he raised his brows.

"Not yet."

I didn't have to say any more. The twinkle in his eyes showed he knew there was only one thing left here for me, one person.

The man who was staying away from me because his mother had killed mine.

What an absolute mess.

When I'd dropped the comment the other day that things were complicated, I didn't know just how tangled the web went. Things weren't complicated then. They were now.

But...what was I supposed to do?

Stop loving Ryan?

Detective Gracen stood and put his hand out to shake mine. "Great to meet you Lana. I really mean that. I hope we won't meet again. I mean that too."

"Thank you for everything. I'm truly grateful." I gave his hand a gentle squeeze. With a curt nod he left.

I stared at the door as it closed and Georgie came out of the kitchen.

"Hey, you okay?" Georgie asked, taking her seat where Detective Gracen had sat.

I nodded. "I will be. I…" I really didn't know what to say. Being asked if I was okay was a normal thing. I got that. It was just that I felt a little like I was lying when I answered and said I was okay because truthfully I really wasn't.

Georgie reached over and took my hands into hers.

"You can say no. You can say no and it will be fine too."

"Then … no. I'm not okay. Every day feels weird. Some parts of the day feel like I got answers so now I can move on. But then there are other parts where I just don't know, Georgie. I really don't know. How do you get through something like this?"

I could still hear the despicable words pouring out of Kathy O'Shea's mouth. I could still see her smiling. That smile of triumph.

She'd won.

She may be in custody now and I was certain justice would be served in accordance with the law but she'd won.

Mama was still dead. All of that didn't bring her

back. *And*, I'd still left Wilmington for seventeen years and Ryan and I never made it as a couple.

The past was the past and it couldn't be unwritten. It was what it was.

"What do you want to do?" Georgie asked.

I sighed and tucked my hair behind my ear. "The only thing I'm sure about is how I feel about Ryan. It's a lot though, Georgie. He's staying away and it makes sense. His father has called to check on me and he's messaged but I can tell the guilt's there."

"Do you blame him Lana?" She drew in a breath and looked at me. "He sees himself as the guy whose mother killed yours. I think that's the part you have to focus on if you want to get through this. The question is, can you see past that part?"

"Could you? If it was you, could you?"

"If we were talking about Pat, then my answer is yes."

"Really?" I wanted to hear this. Hear her reasoning for what she would do. "Would you really?"

"Ryan isn't his mother. He's one person who is separate from everything and he lost out too when he lost you. This whole situation is coming from one vindictive person. That saying is true, *you aren't your family*. So if this was Pat, then my answer would be yes because I know how much my husband loves me, and even when he was just my friend I know that man would move mountains just to see me smile."

That was beautiful and it was true.

There was a truth that resonated with me too. For the first time since I'd met Georgie I felt I could feel that sense of similarity because I had a man who loved me like that too.

The best part of that was knowing it. Knowing the love existed beyond anything and everything.

"I like that." I blinked back a tear. "And it's true, I've witnessed Pat love you to no end."

"Thank you. Lana… you don't need to ask me what I'd do. You know what you want to do. Don't allow the past to get in the way. You're actually sure about the one thing that matters right now. Your love for him. It's a step."

I gave her a little smile and nodded. "When the hell did you get so wise?"

"I have a wise best friend." She gave me one of her sassy shrugs.

Pat stuck his head out from the kitchen and beamed at us with one of his cheeky grins.

"Dinner slash lunch is nearly ready. We could eat together if you're ready to eat in five minutes." He gushed, looking proud of himself.

"I'm ready," I replied. It sounded though like I was

answering for more things than just accepting dinner in five minutes.

We ate and they left a few hours later, leaving me to myself.

By myself with the question of what would happen next pregnant in the air.

Later on I sat outside on the porch swing watching the sunset.

After an hour Ryan's car pulled up on the drive.

My heart sped up when I saw him and it skipped beats when he got out and came over to me.

Before he could even reach me though I rushed to him. It was instinct. It moved me to him.

He held me, hugging me hard to his chest but then he pulled back and released me.

"Hi," he breathed. His eyes scanned over me in that way that showed he was trying to commit me to memory.

"Hi."

He reached out and brushed over my cheek. "How are you feeling?"

"I'm holding up."

"Lana… I'm sorry I haven't been … around. There were a few things I needed to do for my mom. Statements and various other things. Like saying goodbye."

"You said goodbye?"

"Yeah... That was it for me. *Everything*... I don't think I'll ever quite get past it. That's why I'm here."

"Why?"

"It's too much Lana. It's too much... It's all such a messed up story. You deserve better. You always did. You deserve to be with someone pure, who doesn't have the baggage and shit I have." He moved his hand up to his head and paused for a few seconds. "My mother looked at you and told you how she killed your mother. Nothing will ever fully describe how I felt in that moment. Dad is ... devastated and ashamed. He's not sure how he can face her, or you. I had to face you to close the chapter. I love you, and if that is true I have to let you go... This time I truly have to let you go."

His eyes begged me to accept, his words did too, but I wasn't going to.

I was sticking to the answer I kept getting when I thought of what I'd wanted most.

Georgie was right.

The past was the past.

"Maybe it's time to start a new book." I nodded. "The boy and the girl who just wanted to run off together seventeen years ago deserve it."

"Maybe they do... but it's not right."

"It's not about that. Not about right and wrong. We didn't do anything wrong. We had people telling us what was best for us and dictating who deserved better and who didn't. She won Ryan. Your mother won everything else... Please don't allow her to win whatever future we could have."

He gave me an agonized stare. "I don't want you to look at me and remember what she did."

"I don't."

"You say that now, but... it could change Lana. I look in the mirror and I see her son. I'm her son and I can't believe my own mother could be so despicable. I don't want you to look at me and have that memory of who took the person you loved the most away from you." A tear ran down his cheek.

I reached out and touched his face, shaking my head. "Ryan O'Shea, when I look at you I see love."

"How can you?"

"I just do. I see love. I remember the boy who captured my heart from hello, I remember the boy who gave me my first kiss and was my first everything. You filled me with so much inspiration I never had to try to feel. Everything was there and creativity flowed from me because of you. I remember how you always took care of me, how much you wanted to after my mother died, and how I always felt complete when I was with you."

"*Lana...*" he held my gaze.

"It's true Ryan. It's true. I see love when I look at you and I feel loved. Mama wasn't the only person I loved most. There's you too." I swallowed hard and immersed myself in the strength that uplifted me. It was a strength that surprised me. It came from my soul. "My heart is broken in so many ways. We shouldn't allow the actions of our parents to affect us or influence our decisions. I'm choosing you Ryan... I love you."

"I love you too, Lana."

"Then choose me."

He continued to gaze at me, uncertain.

"Ryan O'Shea, choose me. I'm here... and we're the same people, who feel the same way about each other. That has to count for something. Choose me."

It was that simple.

When he nodded my heart soared into the heavens and I actually felt like I would be okay now.

It was the first time I'd felt it in seventeen years.

"I choose you Lana. I... choose you." he bowed his head and when he lifted his gaze to meet mine I smiled and threw myself into his arms.

He held me close to his heart and finally I felt like I was home.

Home.

It was the place that existed wherever he was.

CHAPTER 25

Ryan

Six months later ...

Mom died yesterday...

The news brought me home. Not for her... for Dad.

I stopped in my tracks on the patio, and gazed ahead to the garden where he sat.

He was sitting on the bench Amelia used to sit with Lana. Right next to the climbing honeysuckle vines that covered the archway.

He was just sitting there, gazing out to the pond

where the ducks splashed around as they floated by the lily pads.

Sunshine bounced off dew-bright leaves, making the bursts of color from the flowers Amelia had grown years ago come alive. Roses, sunflowers, Dahlias, hydrangeas.

She'd planted them there and Dad had made sure they were tended to everyday, almost like he was trying to preserve what was left of her.

I continued to watch him, not quite knowing what I'd say. It was a difficult time for so many reasons. So much had happened to create this dark void of a shadow in our lives.

Six months had passed since everything blew up and truth unveiled.

Mom's death felt like this was the seal. That final thing we'd been waiting for to close the chapter

Or maybe it was just me who was waiting.

It was horrible to know the truth of what happened, and still wonder about her.

My mother's illness had gotten to me for so long that it was automatic to think of her first thing in the morning and wonder how she was. It was hard to unlearn the habit.

Hard to accept that she was never who I'd thought she was.

Worse when I truly processed everything she did in my mind.

I'd chosen to be with Lana. I chose to be with her and we were happy. Nevertheless there was a part of me that would always remember the past.

There was a part of me that couldn't just close the book on the past and start a new one. That stemmed from memory and fact. Knowing my family had caused irreparable damage to her.

That was something I'd have to live with for the rest of my life.

Live with it, but I wouldn't allow it to consume me. because it would mean Mom won in every aspect.

Pulling at the air for a cleansing breath I proceeded to walked toward Dad.

He lifted his head when he saw me and I was glad to see his face brighten.

My visit was unexpected.

I lived in L.A now with Lana.

I'd moved and followed her just like I'd planned to when we were supposed to go to New York. We bought a house near the beach and we were happy.

"Hi Dad," I smiled.

"Kid," he breathed. There was a quiver to his voice. It was so unlike him.

I lowered to sit next to him and noticed he held a poetry book in his hands.

"I want to ask how you are, but it feels like a foolish question," I confessed, resting my hand on my knee.

He shook his head. "It's not a foolish question. It's a normal one. I just can't give any kind of answer other than that I'm numb."

Numb was a good word. It summed it up about right.

I felt numb too as a person that had been affected from the truth. He however, must have felt worse than me.

He'd blamed himself for his part in the whole event.

He'd blamed himself to the point where he was currently taking a break from work. That had never happened, and while I would have loved to tell him he shouldn't blame himself, I found it difficult to.

"It was so weird when they called me to give me the news of your mother's passing," he began. "I felt... I felt nothing. It was like the numbness took me and I felt nothing, Ryan."

That was pretty much how I'd felt too when I heard. I always thought the world would stop and I'd crumble when she died. But I felt nothing. I hadn't seen her in six months and I'd decided I wasn't going to. Six months ago really was goodbye.

"It's hard when you feel nothing. It's almost worse," I put in. "Because you know you should feel something."

He agreed. "Ryan, I struggle to feel anything besides

guilt because it really was my fault. All of it. My actions drove your mother to kill Amelia and Amelia is dead because of that."

That was his mantra for the last six months. It was the first thing he'd said when he learned the truth. He'd instantly blamed himself and continued to ever since.

"Dad, you can't keep blaming yourself." It was all I could say to him.

"I just keep thinking, what if I'd served her with the divorce papers earlier, what if I'd done things differently, what if I'd manned up and been forceful in what I wanted… *what if*… It just shouldn't have ended this way Ryan."

"But it did, and what you have to think about is all the steps you did take to make things right. It won't change anything, but it showed you tried." I spoke with a wisdom I never thought I'd have. He seemed to be listening. "We can all feel guilty Dad, but Mom killed Amelia. *Mom*… no one can blame themselves for that part. That is separate to everything because that is her. It's on her. Not you and not me."

A tear ran down his cheek and he quickly wiped it away. He dipped his head and pressed his lips together.

"Thank you for coming."

"I knew you'd need me." I brought my hands together and cracked my knuckles.

"I don't want you to spend too much time away from Lana."

"Don't worry about her. She understands. I …came to help you plan the funeral. I knew you'd find it difficult." It would be difficult for me too, but it was something I felt I should help with. Again for him, not for me, and not for her.

He nodded. "I can't do it. It's the same as living here. I feel like I just can't do it. Living in this house reminds me of the past."

That piqued my interest. "What are you going to do?" I had wondered how he'd manage to cope here. It was hard enough being here myself.

This was actually the place where Amelia was murdered.

"I don't know. There's pain, but there's memories. Good memories. Memories of you growing up, memories of Lana. Memories of Amelia. The house is a part of me. Amelia loved this garden and these are her flowers. It feels like she's here, like a part of her is here. If I don't have that, then it's like she's really gone. But, then there's the other part of this that gets me, because this was the place she was taken from me."

I reached out and tapped his hand. "I don't think it's a decision for now Dad. But I get it. The fact that you're here in this garden means you want to preserve the memory. I think in time you'll know what to do. She's not in the garden Dad. She's in your heart. That's where she lives. You do what keeps that alive for you both."

He gave me a kind smile. "Thank you... I'm proud of you. I'm very proud of you and the man you became." He sighed.

The first real smile of the day inched across my lips. "Thank you Dad."

"You're welcome. You're... no longer a shell Ryan." A lightness came into his eyes that gave me hope he'd be okay. "I'm glad you became the artist and you followed your heart to the girl."

That was exactly what I'd done.

Similar to the past with a few modifications. I bypassed art school and bought a gallery near D'Angelo. Currently I show cased my previous art work and it was doing well. I had plans to do all sorts of things. For the first time in my life I was doing something that felt true to me.

But... I also realized something else. I didn't have to choose. A person who was good at so many things didn't have to choose. It just meant they had a variety of options they could juggle. So I became the artist, but I continued to be the lawyer as well.

"I think I have the best of both worlds."

"I hope so. However, I honestly would prefer if you just focused on art," he admitted.

"I'm good. I am, Dad." I worked with Dad on a

consultancy basis and chose which cases I took on. A majority of them didn't require my presence, just my expertise.

I came back here every other weekend to see Jack. So when I saw Jack, I saw Dad too.

It all worked out in the end. All of it, even with Jack.

The angel that Lana was loved him too and accepted my bond to him, accepted that I was his father and wanted to be part of his life, even if it meant having some element of Tiffany in our lives too. She accepted it.

The agreement was for me to visit Jack, but he'd spend a week with me in the vacation breaks. We'd planned to change things up as he got older.

"I appreciate you, kid." Dad smiled at me.

"You too Dad."

It all worked out.

There was however, one last thing left to do.

One last step I'd never gotten to with Lana to make her mine.

It was the last week of March and the flowers were out in full bloom.

Amelia's graveside looked beautiful with the yellow dwarf roses the caretaker had planted there.

Dad had bought this plot of land at the cemetery for her. By the river and away from everyone else.

There was a garden surrounding the grave filled with Amelia's favorite flowers and a statue of a woman reading a book, a poetry book no doubt.

Dad had all of those made for her for her birthday anniversary a few months back.

Lana and I stood side by side at the site holding hands.

Today was a special visit.

Lana just didn't know it yet.

I'd told her I had to talk with her mom about a few things.

Here we were. This was the first full week we'd been back in Wilmington too so it was perfect.

Things were still very raw, but we were all coping and trying to move forwards with our lives.

I looked at Lana who was giving me one of her glances where she thought she was humoring me.

"Ryan we've just been standing here. Mama would ask you if you were waiting for God to come." She chuckled. "Or, if we were watching for the seasons to change."

I smiled at her. "Yes, I suppose she would." I'd done a good job at keeping her in suspense because we'd been here for a little over half an hour.

"The point is we're waiting," she scuffed.

"Okay, I'm ready. I prepared a speech and everything."

"You are the strangest boy ever."

I nodded, agreeing and she shook her head at me.

I looked back to the grave and my gaze landed on the headstone then scanned over the grave itself.

We could act all we wanted like we were okay and we could smile but the truth lay before us. It lay before me and I couldn't help but remember who put her there.

My mother.

I sighed and forced the memory from my mind. Replacing it with my memories of how Amelia loved me. I remembered my time with her and all she did for me. all the times when I'd felt her love surpassed that of my own mother. I think I was right.

I wished I'd done this when she was alive and could see me. hopefully she could look down from heaven and see me now.

"Amelia," I began with a little smile. "When I was nine I was truly excited to meet you and your daughter. I acted like a little brat because you caught me staring at your girl. When I was twelve I wanted to ask you if it would be okay to take her to the school disco, but I was scared you'd say no because I set fire to her Barbie doll hair, and when I did that I accidentally burned your bible." I looked at Lana who had her eyes glued to me.

Wide. I expected that because this was stuff I never spoke of.

"When I was fourteen I really wanted to ask her to the movies but I thought you'd say no because you caught me stealing shit from the store. By the time I was sixteen I'd gone astray, you tried to keep me focused with my artwork but I never listened. I wanted to ask your daughter to the junior prom but I thought you'd say no because you caught me doing all manner of drugs in the garage. I think I stopped wanting to ask at that point. Two years later a lot had changed and I'd changed too. I think you realized that but you may not have known why. I bypassed you and I was seeing Lana that whole time. There was one thing I wanted to ask you. It was more important than every time I'd wanted to ask you about her. It was this." I fixed my gaze on Lana. "I wanted to ask you if you'd give your blessing for me to ask her to marry me."

"*What?*" Lana gasped.

"At nineteen. I had everything ready. I knew she'd tell my ass to come back to her when I could add twenty years to my age. So the time's about right."

I turned thirty seven last month. At the time I would have asked Lana she was very nearly nineteen and me twenty. I pulled a small velvet box from my back pocket.

Proposing by a gravesite had to be quite original. To

me though I was doing it in front of someone who mattered to the both of us.

Lana gasped when she saw the little box in my hands and brought her hands up to her cheeks when I lowered to one knee.

"In my heart I know she would have said yes. She'd seen me for me, and I know she saw how much I loved you, so here goes the part that counts. Lana, you're the most amazing thing in my life, you always have been. I'd be honored if you'd be my wife. Will you marry me?"

"Yes." She was nodding even before I finished. "Yes... Ryan."

I took her hand and slipped the ring on her finger. It was only once I looked at it on her hand that she felt like mine.

"Thank you." Gratitude filled my soul.

When I stood she hugged me. "I love you, you're the most amazing thing in my life too."

I pulled back and kissed the top of her nose. "It's the prelude to the start of the rest of our lives."

"No," she beamed. "There is no prelude. It simply is."

We both laughed and I pulled her in for a kiss.

It was one that felt different.

It held all our hopes and dreams.

It was the beginning of us.

My girl came back to me and we had a second chance to do all we ever wanted to do.

EPILOGUE

LANA

ONE YEAR LATER...

I always liked this part.

Walking out onto the runway after a show. Especially a show that had gone well and had blown people's minds.

The cheers and applauses coming from my guests were always what got me.

Tonight was no different in that respect.

The runway was surrounded by tiered seating, all

full with people who were now standing and cheering for me as I made my way out.

Guests, models, other designers, friends and family all here supporting me and the dream.

My dream.

I'd been doing this for a while now but things changed up when Ryan came back into my life. I'd look out into the crowd of people and see him sitting on the front row.

My angel. Tonight he was joined by his father who sat next to him and looked equally proud of me. Connor O'Shea looked the same when Ryan and I took our wedding vows five months ago.

Next to them was Georgie and Pat, always and ever there for me.

Tonight was great and similar to most shows I'd had. It was however my first show pregnant, and I had a visible baby bump that people seemed to love all the more in my red dress.

The dress was inspired by my first collection I'd put together in my attempt to apply for the summer school at Parsons.

The dress was called Love.

It was the first time I'd just gone with the emotion because love led me here.

All the people who loved me had brought me to this moment.

I stopped at the end of the runway and looked around, and in my heart warmth surrounded me.

The effulgent glow of the greatest love washed over me when I thought of Mama. It was almost like I could feel her here. In my mind I'd imagined her dressed in her finest just like she used to say. She'd be sitting with my family looking like she'd been pulled from a Hollywood set. I'd look at her as I was doing now with everyone and feel like we'd both made it.

The thought existed in my imagination, but it was real for me.

It was all real for me.

"Thank you all for your tremendous support," I spoke as the cheers faded. "I'm so honored to have you all. Thank you for allowing me to share my dream and vision with you. I value each and every one of you, as always I give credit to my husband."

I focused on Ryan who gazed on at me with that twinkle in his eyes.

"I give him a little extra credit tonight because he's the guy who makes good things great. He turns dreams into realities, memories into legends. He is the keeper of my heart and always has been. I am who I am today because of all that he is to me."

Ryan looked stunned. He wasn't expecting me to do that. I reached out my hand toward him beckoning him to me.

He came. He walked up the steps to the runway and joined me, cupping my face.

"I love you, you know that Lana O'Shea?" He beamed at me.

Lana O'Shea...

I would always relish hearing that.

"I love you too Ryan O'Shea."

The crowd went wild when he bent his head to kiss me, and wilder when he lowered and planted a kiss on my stomach too.

I was happy.

I was happy now.

Love was always the answer to everything.

It brought him back to me, and with him everything else came together to give me what my soul desired most.

THANK YOU SO MUCH FOR READING.
I TRULY HOPE YOU ENJOYED LANA AND RYAN'S STORY.
MUCH LOVE TO YOU ALL XXX

ACKNOWLEDGMENTS

To my readers.
Where would I be without you....
I thank you from the bottom of my heart for all your support,
and for reading my stories.
Hugs and LOVE xx

ABOUT THE AUTHOR

Bella Fontaine is the multicultural and interracial romance pen name of USA Today Bestselling best-selling author Khardine Gray.

The name is to honor the strong, super talented, and courageous women in her family who inspired her to write and do what she loves most.

As with her other books expect hot, steamy, contemporary romance and romantic suspense. Expect drool-worthy heroes and sassy heroines. People falling in love and the wild, sexy fun they have on their journey.

Sign up to her newsletter where you can be spoiled rotten with giveaways and updates on new releases here:

https://www.subscribepage.com/bellafontainebooks

You can find her on Facebook here:

https://www.facebook.com/bellafontaineauthor/

Join the Bliss Romance Hideaway reader group too for more spoilage and fun:

https://m.facebook.com/groups/889377571219117

Happy reading xx

f